Wicked Devouring

Claimed by Gargoyles Book 3

Wicked Devouring
Claimed by Gargoyles, Book Three

SarahPiperBooks.com

Published by Two Gnomes Media

Cover design by Luminescence Covers

E-book ISBN: 978-1-948455-86-2
Paperback ISBN: 978-1-948455-87-9
Audiobook ISBN: 978-1-948455-88-6

BOOK SERIES BY SARAH PIPER

~

M/F Romance Series

Vampire Royals of New York

~

Reverse Harem Romance Series

Claimed by Gargoyles

The Witch's Monsters

Tarot Academy

The Witch's Rebels

GET CONNECTED!

I love connecting with readers! There are a few different ways you can keep in touch:

Email: sarah@sarahpiperbooks.com

TikTok: @sarahpiperbooks

Facebook group: Sarah Piper's Sassy Witches

Twitter: @sarahpiperbooks

Newsletter: Never miss a new release or a sale! Sign up for the VIP Readers Club:
sarahpiperbooks.com/readers-club

CHAPTER ONE

JUDE

If there's anything we can all count on in this life, it's my *complete* fucking inability to follow orders—a condition that's only gotten worse now that my little scarecrow's in the mix.

Thankfully, when it comes to my half-baked schemes and Draegan's oh-so-predictable wrath, Auggie's got a reliable streak, too: my best mate never lets me go up in flames alone.

"You sure you know what you're doing?" he says now, passing me a crowbar and glancing around the quiet, tree-lined street in Bayside, Queens.

Not much happening at this hour.

Not yet, anyway.

"Augustine." I jam the crowbar between the door and the frame, jimmying it until I hear the wood crack. Then, turning to him with a grin, "If self-awareness was a requirement for this job, I'd have been made redundant during the Renaissance. Besides, if Draegan *really* wanted us to leave this bastard alone, he would've told me to do the opposite. 'Go after him, Jude. Do your bloody worst.' Right?"

Auggie runs a hand through his Disney-prince hair and shakes his head. "Your logic. It astounds."

"Precisely why I'm the one holding the crowbar and you're carrying the rope. Now, watch your step and keep your eyes open—these shadow mages can be slippery little fucks."

I push open the door and creep inside, crowbar at the ready. I'm already imagining the wet, satisfying sound it'll make when I embed it in Conrad Nesterman's forehead.

Ah, Connie. Also known as Full Metal Jacket. *Soon* to be known as He Whose Bashed-In Head Adorns the Front Porch Like a Rotting Pumpkin.

Just in time for Halloween season, too. Couldn't have timed it better myself.

Look, it's not as if I do these things *just* to rattle Draegan's cage, as fun as that old pastime may be. After our initial recon of Nesterman's house, he asked us to wait before making another move, and I had every intention of doing just that.

But all that waiting... Fuck. It just makes me twitchy. Every minute these bastards are allowed to draw breath is another minute they could be using their few remaining brain cells to hatch a plan to harm Westlyn.

Not on my watch, dickheads.

We came in through the house's side entrance, and now, with Auggie at my back, we slink through the dark kitchen, our senses immediately assaulted by the fetid stink of old garbage and the sharp tang of cheap weed. Dirty dishes litter every flat surface, and with every step, another roach crunches underfoot.

Another step. Another crunch. A shiver snakes up my spine. I try not to retch.

I fucking *hate* bugs.

"Keep it together, lightweight." Auggie clamps a hand over my shoulder and squeezes, his voice low in the darkness as we make our way out of the dumpster of a kitchen and into the main living area.

More of the same out here, along with some random occult shit scattered around—books, a few Tarot decks, various bottles filled with dark liquid that looks a hell of a lot like blood.

Real home-makers, Connie and his witch-girl, Kelly Obrovski.

No matter. They're both roasting tonight.

The house is narrow, with nothing more than a hallway leading to a bedroom and bath in the back. From behind the closed bedroom door, a series of muffled grunts cuts through the silence, followed by the unmistakable squeak of bedsprings and the sound of flesh smacking flesh.

"Cheeky," I whisper. Then, "You ready to start this party?"

Augs nods. "On three?"

"You bet."

"One—"

I kick down the door in an epic shattering of old wood and cheap veneer.

"Now *that* was satisfying," I announce, swinging the crowbar up over my shoulder.

Two voices shriek—one male, one female—and the pair freezes on the bed.

But me? I'm just trying to process what I'm seeing here.

"What the *fuck*?" Auggie says from just behind me, taking in the sight of the lovely couple whose nightly escapades we've just interrupted—a bloke I assume is Full Metal Jacket, tied to the bedposts in slightly less than Full Metal glory, a spreader bar between his ankles, ball gag shoved into his mouth. And a woman—Kelly, I suppose—dressed in a black thong-and-latex number, straddling him, her arse in his face as she pours hot wax from a lit candle onto his dangly bits.

In the shocked silence that follows, I let out a low whistle. "You make torture look almost fun, mate. And Kelly? Very bold choice, what with the latex around that open flame."

"Uh, Jude?" Auggie says.

"Who knew shadow magic society members were so adventurous? Guess I didn't give you enough credit. Which just goes to show, you can't always judge a—"

"*Jude.*" Auggie grips my shoulder again, his mouth close to my ear. "That's not Kelly Obrovski. It's the fucking doctor. Pomeroy's mother."

"Pomeroy's... Wait. Dr. *Eckhardt*?" I laugh, but yes, now that he mentioned it, I recognize the woman from Rook's surveillance films—the woman we caught leaving Hunter's apartment. "Well. I heard you made house calls, but this is some *special* service you're providing to Connie here. Does Kelly know about this clandestine little romp? Perhaps we should give her a ring."

The suggestion seems to snap them both out of their momentary shock.

Still holding the candle, Eckhardt flings her other hand toward us, likely trying to cast some dark incantation.

Pointless.

Even with my human glamour, I'm faster and stronger and *way* more excited about the prospect of inflicting violence than she seems to be.

I've got her yanked off the bed and shoved against the wall with the crowbar across her throat, one of Rook's dampener cuffs clamped over her wrist before the bitch can even utter another gasp. The candle drops to the floor and sputters out.

Auggie tosses me the rope. While he cuffs our boy, Connie—already restrained, courtesy of the good doctor—I tie the woman to a rickety desk chair and crouch down before her with a grin.

Yeah. *That* grin.

"Time for us all to have a friendly fireside chat," I say softly, patting her knee.

Then I bash it with the crowbar.

Right to the point, this particular instrument. That's what I love about it.

She passes out, naturally.

Connie, however, remains fully aware through it all, moaning and thrashing about like a stuck pig.

Never before have I been so grateful for a ball gag.

Fortunately, it doesn't take long for the doctor to return to us. When she looks up at me again, her eyes are still sharp, but her skin has lost much of its earlier luster; that latex outfit certainly isn't doing her any favors now.

"How's the knee?" I ask. "Looks a bit swollen. Perhaps you should see a doctor?"

Tears spill down her cheeks, but to her credit, she doesn't moan or complain.

"What... what do you want?" she pants.

"Information, naturally." With another grin, I say, "But hey—before we get to the meat of the conversation, quick question... I assume Kelly's in the dark about this, but... does your *son* know you're playing a bit of Fifty Shades with his best mate? Far be it from me to judge, but I feel like that could make birthday parties and family barbecues *really* awkward."

"My... my son?" she sputters, her eyes widening with new fear. "How do you know my son?"

"Jakey? Oh, Jakey and I go *way* back. Alonso, too. Turns out we've all got a mutual acquaintance. A witch by the name of Westlyn Ave—*oh*! I just realized we haven't properly introduced ourselves. How rude of me." I offer a slight bow of my head. "I'm Jude Hendrix, and my associate over there keeping your boy-toy company is Augustine Lamont. Go on, Auggie. Wave to the good doctor."

From his spot beside the bed, Auggie doesn't wave. Just sighs and rolls his eyes. "Fucking *Jude*. Get on with it, for fuck's sake."

Ignoring all this, the doctor says, "Please. My son... Just tell me my son is okay."

I pull my face into a compassionate frown and touch her shoulder. "Your son is okay."

"Really?"

I scoff. "How the fuck should I know? You asked me to *tell* you he was okay, whatever the fuck that means, and I obliged. Now it's time for *you* to oblige *me*."

"Not until I know my son is alive and well."

"Hate to break it to you, Mumsy, but your son was never well. Whether he's alive?" I shrug, recalling the crunchy sound of brittle bones when the meat grinder chewed him up and spit him out the other night—oy, what a racket. "Maybe he is, maybe he isn't. Either way, you've got a choice to make, or you'll never know the answer."

"But... what? What's going on? Where is my son?"

"There, there," I say. "I realize this is a lot to take in, so I'll do you the courtesy of keeping it simple. We need to know *everything* there is to know about the demon Zorakkov, Hunter Forsythe's medical treatments, and why the Forsythes are so keen on binding him to Westlyn Avery. You're in a unique position to connect those mysterious dots for us. So..." I lean in close enough to smell the rubber on her dastardly outfit and whisper, "Cooperation, or pain? Your call, doc."

"Help Jude Hendrix and Augustine Lamont?" Son apparently forgotten, her lip curls into a sneer, her backbone straightening despite her obvious pain. "I would rather *die* than cooperate with the men of shadow and stone."

"Ah, so you *do* know us. Excellent. Well, death is certainly a respectable choice. Unfortunately for you, dying is not one of the options on tonight's menu. Perhaps you should pay closer attention. Here—this should help you focus." I slide a dagger from my boot and jam the blade deep into her thigh—no, not the leg with the shattered knee. The other one. Best to spread the love a bit, I always say.

She grits her teeth. Poor girl must be in *excruciating* pain.

"Looks like I managed to avoid the femoral artery," I say. "But I wouldn't advise any sudden moves. You might nick something vital. Wait, what am I saying? Giving a doctor medical advice? Anyway, I'm sure we understand each other now, don't we?"

Unlike her son, the good doctor doesn't howl like a banshee.

She does, however, give me a nod of surrender, followed by a deep sag of her shoulders and a few tears sliding down those waxen cheeks.

"They'll kill me for this," she whispers, and I know she's referring to the shadow mages.

And steal the fun from under my nose? I don't think so, Mumsy...

"I won't tell them if you don't," I say with a wink.

"No, you don't understand. They'll just... they'll know. They always know."

Connie strains against his bonds, another muffled cry fighting its way around the gag. Auggie gives the bed a swift kick to shut him up.

"Have you two thought about branching out a bit?" I ask our prisoners. "Finding a new friend group? Honestly, these shadow mages sound a bit clingy. Can't be healthy, that level of obsession. Oh! Speaking of unhealthy obsessions! Doctor, have you ever seen what a crowbar can do to a ribcage? Not as precise as a rib spreader in the O.R., of course, but it's quite something, really." I pick it up and admire the curved end. "The trick is getting the proper angle when you first jam it in there, then jiggling it *just* so. Otherwise you risk prematurely splintering the bones and your entire effort is ruined. Anyway! Gosh, listen to me, blathering on about work. I've barely given you a chance to talk." I swing the crowbar up, then bring it crashing down on the windowsill about two inches from her head, taking a nice bite out of the wood. “Right then. Got something to say, doc?”

She nods, fully resigned to her plight. “Cooperation. I... I choose cooperation.”

“Excellent choice,” I say.

And then, the old bird finally sings.

CHAPTER TWO

WESTLYN

Don't fear, little one. Everything is unfolding exactly as it should be...

The voice fades to a soft and eerie echo, and I free-fall into a darkness so black, I'm certain death will be waiting for me at the bottom.

Shouldn't dying be louder, though? More screaming, maybe. Or a sound like the tearing of fabric—a soul being ripped from the body long before its time.

I try to resign myself to it. This quiet leaving. The final breath, the final heartbeat, the last flicker of memories of a life I barely got to experience.

But then...

The thud of another heartbeat.

The rush of new air filling my lungs.

The memory of Draegan's stormy eyes illuminated by the oncoming headlights.

The unmistakable scents of a past I'm still trying to outrun.

Fuel. Metal. Blood.

Fire.

An image flashes through my mind—a Tarot card. A nude woman rising from a black cauldron of flames, a phoenix made of pure firelight bursting free from the depths of her soul.

The Judgement card. A cleansing. Burning it all down and rising from the ashes anew.

The image fades, and the scent of fuel and blood assaults me once more. A cough rattles through my lungs.

Not dead. Not dead. Open your eyes, girl. Open your eyes right fucking now...

Something snaps me to attention—some latent survival instinct that yanks my mind from unconscious oblivion and explodes inside me like that phoenix, burning away the last of the haze.

The moment I open my eyes, pain arcs through my body, blinding and electric. I'm dangling upside down in Draegan's ruined car, suspended by my seatbelt. We must've flipped.

There's a hole where the windshield is supposed to be. A mangled dash and a deflated airbag beneath me. Our car is smashed against the guardrail, and across the oil-slicked road, the car that must've hit us is wedged at a ninety-degree angle between two trees, headlights stacked one on top of the other, shining like twin moons.

A soft breeze rifles through the surrounding trees, followed by the dull hiss of tires slowing on pavement. The ding-ding-ding of an open car door. Footsteps.

Then they stop somewhere behind the car. I can't see anyone.

There's a long pause, and then...

"Yeah, it's me," says a male voice. "It's done. Make your move."

Footsteps again, but this time they're... retreating?

What the hell? Maybe he didn't see me? Didn't think anyone was still inside the wreck?

I know I should cry out for help, but my head is pounding and I can't make my mouth form words and nothing makes sense and then, suddenly, his door slams shut and the car glides past my view, red taillights fading into the black night beyond.

782DSH. The license plate. The last thing I see. The number lodges itself in my skull, like I've just witnessed some impossible crime and need to report it to the police later. 782DSH.

Goddess... Why didn't he help? Who was he talking to? *Make your move?* What move?

And... why isn't Draegan saying anything?

Draegan... The realization slams into me like a fist to the gut, the rest of the night flickering through my memory in rapid-fire playback.

The office. The desk. The bank. The car. The crash.

"Draegan," I finally rasp, slowly turning my head toward the driver's side. "Drae, are you—"

No. No!

He's nothing. He's gone. Just... gone.

Panic seizes my heart, flooding my limbs with adrenaline.

Ignoring the relentless drumbeat in my head, I unhook the belt, drop down, and crawl through the gaping hole where the windshield used to be. Finally out in the street, I stagger to my feet on the pavement, dizziness sweeping over me in hot, sickly waves.

I take a deep breath. Then another. Mentally scan my body, head to toe. Nothing feels broken. Aside from the headache and a few cuts and scrapes, I think I'm relatively okay.

But where the hell is my gargoyle?

Tamping down my rising fear, I head to the guardrail and lean over, peering down into the darkness of a steep ravine, searching for signs of him—a torn piece of clothing, broken branches, tracks, anything.

But it's too dark. I can't make out anything but the vague outline of trees and jagged, rocky outcroppings.

"Draegan!" I call out. "Draegan!"

No response but the endless yawn of that pitch-black ravine. *Damn it.*

He's immortal, I remind myself. *He can't die. Whatever happened, he's fine. He's fine. He's—*

A burst of violet light erupts near the car, and a sudden

warmth fills my chest, wrapping around my heart. I feel a tug deep inside me, and then I'm following it, powerless to resist as it draws me back toward the wreck. Back toward that eerie glow.

For a moment, I wonder if I really did die in the crash, and this is the part where I finally cross over. Am I supposed to walk into the light? Will my mother be there waiting for me?

Will Draegan?

Goddess, no. He can't be dead. Please, please let him be okay...

I take another step, waiting for something to happen. Some instructions or deep inner knowing or—

No. It's not that kind of light.

It's coming from Drae's briefcase in the backseat area. We'd stashed the SSD card and the protection amulet in there as soon as we retrieved them from the safe deposit box. It must be coming from the amulet.

Carefully picking my way back through the wreckage, I find the briefcase still intact, still closed tight. The light dims but still seeps out a bit at the edges. The moment my fingers wrap around the handle, I feel that same odd connection I felt at the bank—the steady pulse, as if I'm holding my own heart in my hand.

Something tells me to keep it close.

With no sign of Draegan, I tighten my grip on the case, cross the road, and head into the woods toward the other car, wondering if I'll find any survivors.

Goddess, they came out of nowhere. And these mountain

roads are so dark and isolated... Shit. We're in the middle of nowhere. I don't even have a phone to call for help or text the guys.

Draegan, where the hell are *you?*

"Hello?" I call out, trying to peer through the windshield, hoping there's more than just a bloodied corpse inside. Hoping they have a phone. "Can anyone hear me in there? Do you need help?"

Before I get a response, another wave of dizziness crests, this one so severe it drops me to my knees. I clutch my head in my hand and close my eyes, willing the nausea to pass.

Come on. Come on. You're fine. You just need—

Footsteps again. Soft. Close. Alive.

Thank the—

"Stand up slowly, Westlyn. And keep your hands where I can see them."

I freeze.

That voice.

That horrid, bone-chilling, nails-on-a-chalkboard voice.

I would recognize it anywhere.

Eloise.

CHAPTER THREE

JUDE

"The Archmage," Belinda Eckhardt begins, her voice weak but her eyes alert. "He and Celine walked the dark path from a very young age. Those of us who knew them back then—well, it was clear they were both natural born leaders destined for great things, but they were still relatively untested among the higher-ranking officials of the shadow magic society. They'd been seeking ways to prove their strength and loyalty when they heard about the plight of the demon prince."

"Zorakkov," I clarify, and she nods, continuing.

"Demonic summoning wasn't new to them—they'd been working with lesser demons for years. So, they formulated a plan that would help the prince, knowing it would also secure their positions in the society."

"Help him what?" Auggie asks.

Still bound to the bed next to him, Connie groans again

—could be a warning, could be a howl of pain. Auggie gives him a swift knee to the ribs to shut him up.

The doctor winces. "Is that really necessary? All this violence, this brutality. It's—"

I grip her jaw and lean in close. "Do *not* lecture us about the necessity of violence and brutality against a coven of witches and mages who think nothing of torturing a young girl and sacrificing countless human lives to bloody demons. The only reason I haven't eviscerated you is that you've got intel I need. Every breath you take is at my discretion, and I'm not the most patient bloke, as you might've guessed. So if you want to keep taking those breaths, I highly suggest you—"

"Jude." Auggie's low warning brings me back from the brink of a complete eruption. My hands are trembling, my hold on her jaw punishing, and when I finally release it, she gasps and spits out a mouthful of blood.

She glares at me, but otherwise doesn't complain.

Fast learner, this one.

"Please," I say, forcing a note of calm into my voice. "Continue this *fascinating* story. And before you think of lying to me or leaving out any of the good bits..." I give the blade embedded in her thigh another twist, making her cry out. "Wouldn't be too hard to nick the femoral artery, would it? And if you die, doc, who would be left to tend to Connie's soon-to-be-acquired wounds?"

The woman swallows hard, then clears her throat. When she speaks again, her voice is fainter.

"Zorakkov... He wanted to attain permanent manifestation on the earthly realm. Without the society's intervention, he could only appear in a severely limited capacity, and never for long stretches of time. He needed a body of his own. One he could inhabit and infuse with his power and immortality—enough to break free of the magic that bound him to hell."

"So they chose a *baby* for this task?" I ask, recalling the story of Hunter Forsythe's adoption. The man may be a grade-A degenerate now, but he wasn't always like that. He was a child once. Innocent, until these monsters got their hands on him.

"Zorakkov is a demon of immense power," she says. "We needed time to mold the perfect human vessel—one strong enough to contain him indefinitely without burning out. The Forsythes knew it would require years—decades, even—to complete the necessary procedures and enhancements. A baby was the only option."

I glance at Auggie, thinking back to what Rook told us about demonic manifestation. They usually need multiple vessels, he'd said, because human bodies are too weak to contain them. They also require a coven of dark witches to help them make the transfer each time without getting trapped in the void between realms, but there's always a risk of getting enslaved by a traitorous coven.

One super-strong human vessel would certainly solve that problem.

"What kind of procedures and enhancements, specifically?" I ask.

The doctor shrugs. "Initially, it was a combination of mental preparation, education about the cause and the magic, and physical training. The child needed to be fully indoctrinated into the society. To learn and appreciate the grave importance of his mission."

"I bet," I say.

"Phase two," she continues. "That's the more intensive phase. Everything from growth hormones to musculoskeletal enhancements to immunity boosters... Age-defying treatments, transfusions, constant monitoring for signs of illness or weakness... There are too many to list, really. Most of them are experimental in nature."

"Experimental medical procedures," I say. "Right. That's when *you* entered the ring, I presume?"

"I was the best candidate for the job. I was a respected society member and a hospital employee with access to everything we needed—equipment, blood for transfusions, tissue samples, bone for grafting, medications. I knew what to do and how to forge the insurance claims, and I believed in what we were working to accomplish. No one else could be trusted with something so crucial to the cause."

Disgust churns in my gut. "Your people adopted a child with the express purpose of turning him into a demonic vessel, subjecting him to mental and physical tortures, experiments... *That's* your cause. You know, I've met some bottom feeders in my day, doctor, but—"

"Oh, no. You've got it all wrong." She shakes her head, clearly ready to defend the Archmage with her dying breath. "It's a great honor to become a vessel—especially one for a demon prince. Hunter was happy to do it."

"At two years old?" I laugh. "Yes, babies are *exemplary* at giving informed consent."

"I meant as he got old enough to understand what his sacrifice would mean for his family, for the society at large. He fully consented to the medical procedures, and he was an adult by then. Nineteen."

I scoff. "Do you hear yourself? It's a wonder they let people like you breed."

She lowers her gaze. "Lennon and Celine... they're good people. You have to know that."

"Oh, of *course* they are!" I look to Auggie, who's watching me with his "get-on-with-it" look. "Augs, I think we should pop over to city hall after this and have a chat with the mayor. See about getting the Forsythes the keys to the city. An honorable mention, at the very least."

"I don't expect you to understand," the doctor says. "You're fae. It's... it's different for witches and mages. We're not supernatural, but we're more than human." Her gaze lifts, watery eyes meeting mine once more. "Do you have any idea what it's like to live with a foot in both worlds, never really fitting into either?"

More than you know.

I look to Auggie again, and for a split second I remember him as he was—my human friend, my neighbor, the bloke who'd take me out for mead and a few laughs at the tavern in town after a hard day's work in my father's fields. No cameras back then—he used to draw and paint. That was his way of capturing the world—a world he saw as beautiful. He was kind and good, full of life, happy.

And now he's here, trapped in a filthy house with filthy people, forced to watch me torture the worst of humanity, just as he's been doing night after night for centuries...

Auggie gives me a single nod, and I know he's thinking about it, too—our old lives. What we lost. What we're still losing, a little more with every sunrise.

I don't even know how much time we've got left.

My fucking heart lurches. This woman believes we're fae because that's what the fae who cursed us intended her to believe. We've spent fifteen hundred years living in forms that weren't supposed to belong to us—weren't supposed to exist. Everyone we ever knew and loved is either dead, or—

I close my eyes, clenching my jaw to keep from lashing out at her again. From telling her the whole gruesome story just so she'll stop feeling so fucking sorry for her pathetic self and her beloved "cause."

"The Forsythes inspired us," she blathers on. "Nurtured our magic, gave us a coven and a family when many would've rejected us. They rid the society of the corruption that was rotting us from the inside out, and turned it into something we could all be proud of."

"Seems to me you've been drinking too much of the coven Kool-Aid," I say.

"Mock me all you want, but—"

"Immortality," I say, cutting her off before I have to hear anymore odes to the Archmage. "That's what you're trying to achieve with Hunter. How? Even for a pureblooded mage child—which Hunter was *not*—how the fuck is something like that even possible?"

"It isn't. Not really. Our procedures don't make him immortal, they merely make him stronger and less vulnerable to human disease, injury, and natural aging. Once the demonic entity has taken full possession, the vessel bonds with the demon's immortal essence until they are virtually one and the same." Her eyes glow with some newfound awe. "It's quite amazing to see. The applications for human medicine are—"

"Yes, I'll be sure to mention that to the Nobel committee when I submit your nomination. You're still treating him, then?"

She gives me a wary glance.

"We've got surveillance footage of you coming and going from his apartment," I say. "So if you're not treating him, perhaps you're..." I thumb over toward Connie. "Making one of your special house calls?"

A huff of irritation, then, "I was... concerned about him. Hunter has not been the same since his bride—"

"Do *not* call her that," I seethe. "And spare me your false concern for Hunter. Hunter was a child that you and your lot murdered. All that's left is a shell you've filled with a vicious demon."

"You don't understand. I—"

"Why didn't the medical treatments start until Hunter turned nineteen?" I press. "Why not sooner?"

After everything she's already shared, this seemingly innocuous question seems to shut her down. Her lips press into a thin line, the last of the color draining from her face.

On the bed, our other prisoner tries his luck again, arching his back, thrashing his legs, groaning in frustration and fear. Whatever the answer to this question, it's clear he doesn't want her to tell us.

"Augustine?" I say, nodding at poor Connie. "Perhaps the Yankee Candle needs his wick dipped again."

There's a lovely selection of candles in all shapes and sizes on the bedside table, and Auggie selects a nice, fat red one, along with a lighter.

I turn my attention back to the doctor, but before I can prod her to continue, Connie's back at it with another fit of hysterics.

I glance over at Auggie, who's diligently passing the dripping red candle over the man's unmentionables.

"Guess he likes it better when you do it," I say to the doctor. Then, raising my voice to be heard above the ruckus, "You were saying?"

"Stop!" she cries. "You're hurting him! You're—"

I grip the handle of the dagger and give it another good twist.

"My associates and I have hurt a great *many* shadow mages, doctor," I say darkly. "And something tells me we'll be hurting a great many more before this ordeal reaches its end. Some of these mages may even be familiar to you. *Very* familiar. So perhaps you might spare a few more thoughts for your son instead of worrying about the boy-toy strapped to the bed."

The alarm in her eyes spikes. "Where's my son? Do you have him?"

"The *treatments*." I unhand the dagger. "Why the delay?"

She unleashes a breath. Sweat beads on her skin, and a fresh trickle of blood runs down her thigh.

"We... we had to wait for the... the birth," she pants. "The birth is what set everything in motion."

A sickening heat roils in my gut as the pieces click into place.

I already know the answer to my next question, but I ask it anyway.

"The birth of *whom*?"

CHAPTER FOUR

AUGUSTINE

At Jude's question, the woman lifts her head. A beatific smile dawns on her pale face, chasing away the apparent concern for her son.

I tip the candle upright, afraid I won't be able to hold it steady once I hear Westlyn Avery's name spill from the vile bitch's mouth.

I suck in a deep breath. Set the lit candle on the table. Count the mouse droppings scattered behind it, just to keep from launching myself at the woman and ripping out her tongue at the mention of our witch.

But when she finally speaks again, it's not Westlyn's name on her lips at all.

"The Moon Blessed," she whispers reverently, her eyes taking on the unmistakable blissed-out sheen of the truly brainwashed. "The Peacebringer."

It takes my mind a minute to catch up with the words —*Moon Blessed? Peacebringer?*

Jude cocks his head. "Moon Blessed? What the *fuck* are you on about? The—"

"I'm not saying another word until I've got proof my son is alive," she snaps. The blissful haze evaporates, her eyes crackling with new ferocity. Mama bear mode, activated.

For all the good it will do her.

"Your son," Jude hisses, and I know from the rage in his voice I've got about five seconds before he grabs his crowbar and splits her skull.

"*Jude*." I jerk my head toward Conrad, still moaning incoherently on the wax-splattered bed. "Why don't you come over and chat with our Yankee Candle. I'd like a few moments with the good doctor, if you don't mind."

He glowers at me like I'm the mean dad putting him in timeout, but then he blows out a breath, drops the crowbar, and joins me by the bedside.

I grip the back of his neck and lean in close, searching his face.

"You good?" I whisper.

"I keep thinking about our girl, Augs," he says softly. "What they fucking did to her—all of them. That woman is just as guilty, even if she never laid a hand on West directly."

"And she'll pay. Soon. We just need to figure out what else she knows, okay?"

"Yeah. Yeah, I'm good. See what else you can get out of her." He nods once, then hops on the bed beside Conrad, giving him two swift smacks on the chest. "Just us now, Connie. You and me."

I cross the room and crouch down in front of the woman, the stench of blood and fear wafting off her.

"Jacob is a good boy," she mutters, like she's trying to appeal to my humanity. Like she thinks I have any left to appeal to. "Please. He's always been good. My son is—"

"Your son," I grit out, unable to even say Pomeroy's name, "was a vicious animal in whose prolonged, agonizing mutilation my associates and I took the *greatest* of pleasures."

"You're lying!" she cries. "Take me to him. I'll tell you anything else you want! Just... just let me see my son!"

"You want to see your son? Fine." I pull out my cell phone and scroll through the shots from that night—the few I'd taken on my phone.

Even now, the memory of Westlyn's viciousness makes me hard. She fucking took them *down* for what they did to her.

But then I remember the runes. The terror in her eyes when she realized what she'd done. The shame and confusion.

I remember how she shook with that same terror and shame the night we saw her scars, and all the tears that fell from her eyes when she told us what they'd done to her as a kid.

Fury boils inside me, making my hands tremble just as Jude's did moments earlier.

There is no room for compassion. No room for decency.

I find a nice closeup shot—one that leaves no doubt whatsoever about Pomeroy's condition—and hold it up for her to see.

"By the time we finished with him and Florentine, there was barely enough left of their bodies to burn. Your son was pretty much liquified—see that?" I scroll to another photo, this one of the grinder. The blood spilled on the ground around it. "It was harder to clean up than you'd think. Even with a power-washer. If you'd like, I could head over there, see if I can scrape up a bit of—"

"Stop. Please, just... just stop." Her ferocity is gone. Her shoulders slump, the pain of her sudden grief—not to mention the dagger in her thigh and the destroyed knee—clearly too much to bear. Her eyes drift closed, and she pants for breath, her chest rising and falling rapidly. I can hear the frantic beat of her heart. She's losing more blood. Losing hope.

Good.

I put my phone away and grab her by the hair. "Cry and beg all you want, doc, but the only family reunion in your future is happening at the gates of Hell. But before I send you there, I've got a few more questions about the demon binding. Specifically, why Westlyn Avery is so important to—"

"No. No!" Her eyes fly open again, some new energy exploding inside her. Blood trickles from her nose, her mouth, and she wrenches her head free from my grasp, glaring at me with wild eyes. "You can't stop the great purging! Not even the men of shadow and stone, no! It was set in motion long ago and will continue on its course until all the ancient wrongs have been righted. Until the balance is restored. Death to all who oppose the scourge. Death to all who stand in the way of our rise to power!"

I grab Jude's crowbar and lift it menacingly. "Stop screaming, or I'll—"

"Death!" she shouts, loud enough to send the roaches scurrying out from the shadows. "Death to all who refuse to kneel before the two great lords!"

And with that final trip on the crazy train, the good doctor bends forward and smashes her chest against the hilt of the dagger in her thigh.

Blood gushes from the wound. Way too much of it.

"Fuck!" I shout. "She just fucking severed her own damn artery!"

I cast around the filthy room for something to stop the bleeding, to prolong her worthless life a few more minutes —just long enough to answer my questions about West.

But it's too late.

She's going, going... *gone*.

I toss the crowbar to the floor. "Damn it."

"Don't sweat it, Augs," Jude says, leaving Connie to join me in front of Dr. Corpse. "Bitch was getting annoying at the end there, wasn't she? Pretty sure she wasn't going to share any more details about the whole thing, anyway."

"Probably not." I shove a hand through my hair,

suddenly wanting nothing more than to burn the whole place to the ground and wipe it out of existence.

Jude clamps a hand over my shoulder. "Let's say we wrap things up and get the fuck out of here, yeah?"

"We're not gonna question Conrad?"

"Oh, I tried. Had a nice, intimate little one-on-one with him. But it was all just blubbering and begging, blubbering and begging, and frankly, I'm not in the mood for any more whining tonight." He steps around me and grabs the crowbar. "Just need another moment with the good doctor, here. I've got a vision for my next art installment."

"Great," I deadpan. "I can hardly wait for the big reveal, Michelangelo."

"Do me a favor—look in the closet and see if you can find a backpack or a gym bag—something I can carry a few things in."

I rummage through the closet and find an old duffel, then toss it on the ground at his feet. "Get it done, Jude. The stench in this place is giving me a fucking headache."

Jude flashes his psychotic, fucking-Jude grin, and I watch in silence as he gets to work relieving Dr. Belinda Eckhardt of her ribs.

It's nothing I haven't seen before. A hundred times. A thousand. I've lost count of the people we've tortured, killed, eviscerated. De-boned.

But it weighs on me tonight in a way I've never felt before—or maybe just never noticed—and now it hits me, all at once, that I'm standing here in this shithole house that smells like garbage and blood and candle wax, watching my best friend crack apart a woman's ribcage for one of his twisted sculptures, and every fucked-up thing in my life and his for the last fifteen hundred years can be traced back to the dark fae. To the curse. To all the lives and hope and possibility and fucking humanity those bastards fucking stole from us.

And there's Jude, elbows-deep in a dead woman's chest cavity, hands covered in blood and gore, and... *Fuck*. He used to be the guy who jumped in to *stop* the fights, the one who'd take a drunkard's fist to the gut to save some other poor bastard from the same fate. The one who'd stay at the tavern long after closing just to make sure the woman who ran the place could finish up her night without being harassed.

He was always a little crazy—that's just Jude. But he was also funny and kind and he loved fiercely—his family. His friends. Strangers he'd invite to the table to share a meal.

We all did.

But that's gone now. All of it. Because that's what tragedy does to us. Violence begets violence begets violence. A river of blood becomes an ocean, and it's never fucking enough. Not until you're the last one standing, soaked in it, watching the remains of humanity burn down around you and you finally realize there's not a soul left to help you celebrate your hollow victory.

Jude gets to his feet and hands over the blood-soaked duffle. "Hang on to this. Something else I need to do."

He heads for the bed, where Conrad is barely clinging to consciousness, and grabs the still-burning candle off the table, using it to light the others.

Then he leans over the mage and says softly, "I'm sure you have a safe word, Connie. But since I can't understand a fucking thing coming out of your mouth, it won't do you much good. Anyway, you really shouldn't leave these candles unattended. Says so right on the label."

With that, he touches the flame to the sheets.

"This is for Westlyn Avery," he says calmly. "The girl you couldn't destroy. She's stronger than you ever gave her credit for. Stronger than you and your so-called friends and all the dark magic in your arsenal."

It takes a minute for the fire swirling at the edge of the bed to finally reach Conrad Nesterman's flesh, but when it does...

Fuck, the sound that he makes... The stench of his hair and skin being consumed by that fire...

Acrid smoke clouds the room, making me gag.

Jude looks at me. Nods once. I nod in return.

We're done here.

Leaving the two corpses to burn, we head back out the way we came and slip into the shadows across the street, watching until the house is completely engulfed and neighbors begin wandering out of their homes. Sirens wail in the distance, but it doesn't matter. By the time the firetrucks arrive, there won't be anything left for them to salvage.

Wordlessly, Jude takes the duffel from my hand and hauls it over his shoulder.

We're about to make for the skies when a cold, invisible force explodes inside me, doubling me over. It feels like glass in my lungs, like fire in my gut, like all the worst of those so-called heebie-jeebies crashing down on me at once.

"Jude," I breathe, and he spins around to face me, his eyes going wide as he takes in the sight.

He puts a hand on my back and crouches down to meet my eyes. "Augs. What's going on, mate? You suck in too much smoke?"

"It's... It's West. I can feel it."

"What do you mean? How?"

"I don't know what the fuck happened, but I think she's in trouble." A wave of nausea barrels over me, and I turn my head and wretch, barely missing his shoes. "Call... call Drae," I bite out. "Something is off. Way the fuck off."

CHAPTER FIVE

WESTLYN

"Eloise," I breathe, my voice thin. I open my eyes, hoping against the odds that I've only imagined that shrill tone, that thinly veiled disgust.

But there she is. Beady eyes lasering in on me, lips curled in a perpetual sneer, not a single hair out of place.

My stepmother.

"But..." I blink, still not ready to accept the fact that she's real. That she's here, hours away from the city, days away from where Rook last tracked her and my father. "How did you—"

"Have you been away from us so long you've already forgotten how shadow magic works? Honestly, Westlyn. The way your father raised you... It's a wonder you've even managed to feed and bathe yourself without us. Although, judging from the state of your hair, I'm not sure bathing has been a priority—"

"Shadow magic? But you'd have to know my location first. I'm nowhere close to home. I'm not even—"

Make your move...

The words echo ominously.

The man in the street. The phone call.

That's why he didn't look to see if there were survivors.

He wasn't there to help us.

He was there to help coordinate the attack.

"This... this wasn't an accident," I stammer.

Eloise lets out a cruel laugh. "Got it all figured out now, have you? Well. Aren't you a clever girl?"

"Apparently not clever enough."

"Oh, for Morrigan's sake. Did you really think you could outrun this forever? Your obligations? Where is your sense of honor, Westlyn? Your family loyalty?"

"You are *no* family of mine."

"And you are no match for the shadow magic society or for your future husband, who is none too pleased with you." She holds out her hand toward me and lifts her brows expectantly, as if she might actually shame me into taking it.

As if I'm some wayward little girl who's spent the last hour hiding from her mother in the woods, but now I'm all tuckered out and ready to go home and deal with the consequences of my bad choices.

"Not on your fucking life." I finally get to my feet, sucking in a breath of cool air to stave off the nausea. I'm still clutching the briefcase, but if Eloise finds my choice in post-crash accessories odd, she doesn't mention it.

Just rolls her eyes at my very existence.

Good to know some things never change.

"No more games, girl. You've given the Archmage enough trouble with your cut-and-run act." She clucks her tongue. "Shacking up with fae mobsters."

"They're not—" *fae*, I almost say, but she doesn't know that. She *can't* know that. "Mobsters," I finish up.

"What would you call a pack of wild fae who prey on the naiveté of a helpless witch? As if the men of shadow and stone could protect you from your destiny—it's laughable, Westlyn. Truly laughable. All they've managed to accomplish is to put themselves on the top of the society's hit list. I hope you weren't too..." She flashes a cruel, cutting smile. "*...attached.*"

Guilt simmers inside, knowing I've put them at risk. But I refuse to rise to her bait.

I need to get away from her.

I cast around for a weapon—a rock, a stick—but all I've got is Drae's briefcase.

"Still clinging to hope, are we?" She frowns at me and shakes her head as if even in the moment of my inevitable capture, she's still disappointed in me. "Time's up, Westlyn. Come. We have much to discuss, and weeks of lost time to make up for. You're lucky the Archmage still wants you alive—you have *me* to thank for that, of course. But that's contingent upon your cooperation."

"You don't have it. You will *never* have it." I take a step backward, clutching the briefcase to my chest like a shield, trying to calculate my chances of making a run for it.

Maybe I could lose her in the woods. Find a cave, or...

"Don't bother," she says, knowing exactly where my mind has gone. "These woods are nothing but shadow, and I'm—"

I launch the briefcase at her, and her hands fly up to protect her face. In that split second of distraction, I turn and bolt into the woods, not caring that I've just lost the only clues my father left me about my life.

None of those clues will matter if Eloise catches me—I won't *have* a life after tonight.

My feet pound against the forest floor, sending bolts of pain up my legs, every thud reverberating through my skull. I don't dare turn around, don't dare stop to catch my breath or orient myself.

I just run.

And run and run and run...

Smack into the very woman I'm so desperate to escape.

Fucking shadow magic. Shit!

Cruel fingers tighten around my arm, her other hand yanking on my hair and pulling tight—so tight it makes my eyes water.

"I've spent decades working on this!" she hisses. "Decades ensuring every detail was perfect. You will *not* ruin this for me!"

I claw at her face, wishing I had that dagger from the meat packing plant. Wishing I could carve her up with pretty moonlight runes, just like I carved up those fucking mages—mages that she sicced on me when I was a kid.

The memory of their tortured screams calls to something deep and primal inside me, the scent of their blood stirring a desperate hunger back to life...

The back of my neck burns—the very spot where the fae rune showed up in Auggie's photos—and another Tarot card appears in my mind. Not Judgement this time, but the Tower. The same card I saw the night we killed the mages, right before Draegan took me to the Ryker plant.

And just like that night, the same otherworldly voice echoes through my mind.

Upon those screaming hours
Bathed in blood and breath
You will give them light, my moon
And I will give them Death.

With newfound strength, I kick Eloise's legs out from under her and knock her to the ground, straddling her and wrapping my hands around her throat.

That wild hunger roils inside me, connecting with a power so ancient it must be even older than the trees that surround us. Yet somehow, it feels impossibly familiar to me, like a beloved flannel shirt worn soft in all the right places, or a favorite old song whose lyrics I've only just remembered.

Silver and violet light bursts from my hands, and Eloise

shrieks like a cat in heat beneath me, thrashing and writhing, but I don't let go.

Sparks of magic sizzle across her skin where I touch her, hot and electric, unleashing a flood of images in my mind—a maternity ward full of crying babies, one of them boasting a head of black-and-silver locks. My father's young face, pale and bewildered as someone puts that child in his arms. The bullies who tormented me throughout my young life. Zorakkov on the cathedral altar, slicing my palm. The dark fae male from my nightmares. All the shadow mages and witches from my wedding night, now hooded and robed, summoning legions of demons from the very bowels of hell.

Throngs of people cowering before them. Chained. Whipped. Stripped and marched through the streets of Manhattan, executed in the most gruesome, dehumanizing ways.

And fire. So much fire.

Eating, consuming, absolutely *devouring* everything in its wake until there's nothing left of the city's infamous skyscrapers but the ground on which they were built.

The images are like some dark, twisted brew of all my worst memories and nightmares, so vivid and raw I can't help but wonder if Eloise is somehow rooting around in my mind, fishing out all of my darkest fears.

But as soon as the thought forms, I know it isn't true.

These visions don't belong to me at all.

They're hers.

Not nightmares and fears, but... hopes. Achievements. Her carefully executed plans leading to her perfect future.

Goddess, whatever this strange magic is, it's allowing me to tap into her thoughts. To read her like one of Rook's library books.

Still struggling to break my grip, Eloise gasps, her eyes widening with shock. Then, as quickly as they flooded my mind, the images go black.

She must've realized what was happening, and now she's shielding her mind from me—another shadow magic trick.

"What the fuck is *wrong* with you?" I whisper, the magic inside me receding, leaving nothing but horror in its wake. "*That's* what you're working for? A world where—"

Her fist rockets toward me, glancing off my jaw.

Eloise uses the distraction to shove me off her. I land on my back, jaw throbbing. Stars dance before my eyes. My mouth fills with the coppery taste of blood.

Damn it, girl. Get up. Get up and fight!

I think of the runes again. The dagger. The Tower card and the verse... but I'm totally tapped out. The headache is back with a vengeance, my limbs trembling with exertion.

Eloise can't be fairing much better, though. I hear her wheezing as she struggles to her feet.

Her magic must be running on fumes, too, or she would've nailed me by now—my temporary power surge notwithstanding.

I force myself to stand on wobbly legs. I've just

convinced myself to make another break for it when a bolt of harsh yellow magic splits the darkness before us. Four cloaked mages spill out of the shadows.

"Fuck," I mutter.

"Language, Westlyn." Eloise is on her feet again, too, casually picking leaves from her hair. To the mages, she says, "I gave her the chance to come willingly. She refused. No need to be gentle, but do keep her alive."

The mages surround me. Two of them grab my arms, the other two my legs, rough hands jerking me right off the ground.

"Let me go!" I scream and kick and buck with the last of my strength, but their hold is too fierce. Brutishly, they carry me back to the scene of the crash, Eloise sauntering ahead of us like a fabled queen leading her faithful guards. I'm sure she's got a car waiting further up the road—I'm not a shadow mage, so they can't portal me through the shadows.

For the first time since I escaped my doomed wedding, a sense of true dread stabs my gut.

I try again to kick free, but it's useless. I'm exhausted. My vision is swimming. I've got four shadow mages and my evil bitch stepmother taking me prisoner.

I have no idea if my father is involved. If he knows what his wife is doing to me. If he even cares.

My thoughts drift again to Draegan.

He'll be here. He's always here when I need him. He's fine. Everything's fine...

"Stop mumbling, girl." One of the mages tightens his grip, digging into my arm.

"Struggle all you want," Eloise calls over her shoulder. "You can't stop this any more than you can read a Tarot card or cast a spell. Your only job now is to help ensure everything the *rest* of us have worked for comes to pass."

"I will *die* before I help you," I hiss.

She doesn't even spare me another glance. Just waves her hand around like she's shooing a fly. "Enough, Westlyn. It's been a long night. No need to add your dramatics to the—"

Her words evaporate as a disturbance overhead has everyone glancing skyward.

I follow their worried gazes, and my heart soars.

My sweet ravens—along with several dozen of their friends—swoop down en masse from the treetops.

"Not again with these fucking *birds*!" Eloise frantically swats the air as Lucinda dives for her face. My girl gets in a good gouge to the bitch's cheek before taking off again, only to circle back for another attack.

The mages drop me on my ass, turning their attention to the swarm that's rapidly descending, sharp beaks and talons bared.

But those shadow mage assholes are about to have *much* bigger problems than my feathered friends.

Behind them, a dark figure rises from the shadows—a colossal winged beast wreathed in moonlight, fangs and claws glinting like knives, those unmistakable storm-ravaged eyes blazing with a thirst for blood.

Mage blood.

Tears of relief spill down my cheeks, and despite my pain, I smile.

Draegan.

CHAPTER SIX

ROOK

Alone in the Blackmoor library, the crackling fire and familiar stacks of ancient tomes my only company, I'm deep into a book on demonology and summoning theories when I feel it.

Like a cool breath on the back of my neck, or a subtle shift in the earth not quite strong enough to rattle the windows, but just enough to leave me unbalanced.

Goosebumps ripple across my arms, and I rise from the table, abandoning the demonology book to go investigate.

Nothing seems amiss in the barn—main room, loft, kitchen, bath, everything is quiet. Nothing odd on the security feeds either. But the moment I step outside, the ominous feeling intensifies.

The night is so silent and still, it feels as if every living creature has abandoned this place.

No crickets. No bats. Not the hoot of an owl or even a chill autumn breeze to rustle the apple trees.

And no ravens, either.

What the hell?

I could've sworn they were with me in the library earlier. Generally, they come and go as they please, but they never fly far from the property, always sticking close even when West isn't around.

"Huxley?" I call out. "Lucinda?"

Nothing. Not so much as a distant squawk or flap of black wings over the orchard.

I'm about to chalk it off to an overactive imagination spurned on by the demonology deep-dive, but the moment I turn back toward the library, a bright burst of light explodes inside.

Fire? Fear grips me in a tight fist, and I barge back in through the doors, desperate to put it out before it devours my entire collection.

But it's no fire.

It's... Holy shit. It's the Cerridwen Codex.

It's open, light emanating from its pages like a sunrise cresting over the table.

A shiver runs down my spine, dread sinking deep in my gut. We've been trying to crack this thing open ever since we stole it from Forsythe. I should be celebrating, but this? No. Something isn't right. I can feel it.

I approach it slowly, as if the thing's a wild animal poised to strike, because that's exactly the energy it's giving off. As soon as I get close to the table, the light changes to a deep violet. Tiny lightning bolts arc across the pages. It's like it's warning me to stay back.

And then the wind starts up. For a second I think I've left a door open, but no. This damn book seems to be generating its own weather system.

The wind picks up in earnest, sending my demonology notes scattering across the other table. I scramble after them, gathering everything up as best as I can before another gust hits, whipping my hair around my face, sending books toppling from the shelves.

What the fuck is going on with this thing?

I stash my research in a kitchen cupboard and make my way back toward the Codex, fighting against the increasing rage of the storm. Within seconds, the harsh wind turns vicious. Books and pieces of computer equipment sail past me, swept up in a strange magical tornado.

Curling my wings around me to avoid a direct hit to the face, I stretch out a hand and reach for the Codex. My fingers brush the outer edge, and a painful spark shoots up my arm. Another try, another shock, this one worse than the last. I dare to take another step closer, but it's like the damn thing senses my intentions—it smashes me with a gust of wind so intense, it knocks me on my ass.

I spot my tablet on the ground and snatch it up, then drag myself back outside, slamming the door shut on the Codex and its freaky magic.

Winded, I smash out a group text to the boys—*Codex*

just cracked itself open. Damn thing won't let me get near it—unleashed some kind of magical storm INSIDE the library. Bad feeling about this one. You guys all okay? Get your asses home!

Auggie responds immediately. *Something's definitely wrong—we felt it too. Last heard from Drae when they left the bank hours ago. Can't reach them now. Sit tight—Jude & I are heading out from Queens to search the roads & highways. Keep trying Drae's phone and let me know if you hear anything.*

Will do, I reply. *Keep me posted.*

Fuck.

We disabled tracking on all our devices—in our line of work, it's not wise to risk anyone hacking the system and pinpointing our locations or discovering who we might've come into contact with. I was supposed to find a secure alternative that would allow us to track each other at any time without the risks, but that project fell by the wayside.

We never needed it—we always knew, at least roughly, what the others were up to. Before West came into our lives, our biggest day-to-day worries were dodging the feds, keeping the city's corrupt officials in our pockets, and fending off the odd vampire or two who wandered onto our property in search of a midnight snack.

This scenario was never supposed to happen. We're the only living gargoyles in existence. We stick together and check in frequently, even when we're driving each other crazy. We don't ignore calls and texts. We don't change plans without letting someone know. And we don't go off-grid unless... unless something terrible happens.

Something that leaves us no other choice.

Fear hovers close, but before it overtakes me, my logic kicks in.

Do something, Rook. Take a deep breath and fucking do something.

Forcing myself to stay calm, I check the security systems again, the wards, even the manual locks on all the doors and windows in the manor—everything is as it should be. I speed through the video feeds on my tablet again—nothing is amiss, inside *or* outside. For good measure, I do a manual perimeter sweep around the entire property, searching every shadow and dark corner for signs of trouble. I even take to the skies for an aerial view, circling Blackmoor several times to be sure.

Other than the tornado in the library, there's nothing so much as a damn blade of grass out of place.

An hour later, I still haven't been able to reach Drae. Jude and Auggie aren't responding, either.

Grabbing a broom from the manor, I decide to try my luck with the Codex again—if I can knock it to the ground, I might be able to slam it shut before my precious library is completely demolished.

Assuming the damn thing doesn't kill me first.

But the moment I enter the barn, the unnatural wind just... dies. Equipment I was certain I'd find in ruins simply returns to its original positions, seemingly undamaged. Books re-shelve themselves before my eyes. The ominous purple light dissipates, the library swathed in all-consuming darkness but for a few embers still glowing in the fireplace.

And then, with a quiet, unassuming hiss at complete odds with the tempest that erupted earlier, the Codex snaps shut.

CHAPTER SEVEN

DRAEGAN

Westlyn. Get to Westlyn.

From the moment I opened my eyes at the bottom of that ravine, I had one mission. One mantra that kept me going, despite the pain.

Fucking get to Westlyn.

I'd been in my human glamour when we crashed, and I wasn't wearing my seatbelt. The injuries I sustained would've killed an actual human, but for me, it just meant being stuck with the glamour until my body regained enough strength to call up my true form without causing more damage.

Unfortunately, I didn't have the luxury of resting and waiting it out. I had to find Westlyn. I had to make sure she was all right.

The climb up the steep ravine was excruciating. I'm fairly certain I broke a few more bones on the arduous trek.

Somewhere along the way, however, my glamour loosened its grip, finally setting the gargoyle free.

And now, with little more than a blinding headache remaining, I finally crest that impossible fucking rise.

My car is a mangled heap mere inches from the guardrail, the windshield completely gone, which explains my epic launch into the stratosphere. But Westlyn... No. She was wearing her seatbelt. I know she was. She couldn't have been ejected from the car. Which means...

My heart nearly fucking stops. She's trapped in there. She's been trapped in there this whole time, and she's not making a sound.

Please, please let her be alive...

I hold my breath as I approach, my heart in my fucking throat, every step sending another bolt of fear shooting through me...

But she's not in the car. I can see the airbags deployed on impact. Her belt was unhooked. She must've gotten out, but where the hell could she possibly—

A flurry of movement overhead catches my eye, and I glance up.

Ravens and crows. Dozens of them. Hundreds, even. They're heading into the forest across the road, where I now see the car that hit us, wedged between two trees.

And just beyond it, Westlyn.

The breath leaves my lungs in a great sigh of relief, but it's short-lived.

She's alive, thank the fucking devil, and I'm already on my way to her.

But four men—four fucking *mages*—have their hands on her.

No. Not happening.

The birds swoop in for the attack. Westlyn falls to the ground in the mages' rush to defend themselves, and I'm there a heartbeat later, nothing but a blur of claws and fangs and gore as I grab the closest mage and cleave open his chest, not caring that the others can see my true form.

They won't be leaving here tonight anyway.

"Draegan," Westlyn breathes, and I want to weep at the sound of it, at the confirmation that she's still indeed alive. But there's no time. I grab another mage by the throat, the others fleeing deeper into the woods as the birds continue their assault, confusion and chaos making the men stupid.

"P-please! Whoever... whatever you are... I..." The bastard lifts his hands in surrender. His hood falls back, revealing a pale face and wide, frightened eyes. He can't be more than twenty. "I was just following orders. I—"

I cut him off with a cold laugh. "Sorry, are you under the impression you get to live after putting your hands on her? That there's even a *chance* you're walking away from this?"

"But I just—"

I smash a fist through his chest and tear out his warm, wet heart. He's still gasping as his body drops to the ground and I pitch the organ into the woods.

Let the coyotes fight over it.

I turn to Westlyn, offering a hand to help her up. "Are you hurt?"

"I'm... I'm okay. Draegan, Eloise—she's with them too."

Fresh panic floods my limbs.

"Stay here." I give her shoulder a quick squeeze. "I'll be right back."

I hate leaving her again, but I've got no choice. I need to hunt those mages down and *end* them.

No sign of Eloise yet, but I find the males easily. They haven't gotten very far, still dodging attacks from the birds, their faces raw and bloodied. One of them is missing an eye.

I take One-Eye down easily, tackling him to the ground and tearing out his throat. The second bastard tries to put up a fight, but he's no match for me, either. He thrusts a hand toward me as if to cast a spell, but I grab it easily, wrenching his arm behind his back. I shove him face-first into a tree, bashing his head repeatedly until it's little more than pulp.

Taking a moment to catch my breath, I cock an ear and listen for Eloise.

The woods have fallen silent. The birds are gone. I hear nothing but a faint breeze through the treetops.

Damn it.

I head deeper into the woods, looking for signs of her, but there's nothing. Not a trace. It's as if she just vanished, or...

Fuck. Shadow magic. Westlyn.

I bolt back to the spot where I left her, but she's gone.

You fucking idiot, Caldwell. You never should've left her.

"Westlyn!" I call out. "Westlyn!"

Where the *fuck* is she? I swear to the devil I will tear every fucking tree out of this fucking forest if—

The breeze shifts, carrying her scent to me—apples and sweetness, a hint of leather. All of it mingled with the unmistakable scents of gasoline and burned rubber.

She must be back at the wreck.

Exiting the woods, I finally spot her.

"Westlyn, thank the fucking stars. Are you—" I stop abruptly. Something isn't right.

She appears unharmed, but it's like she doesn't even see me. She's standing in the middle of the road, arms outstretched, eyes glassy and wide, utterly entranced. In one hand, she's clutching my briefcase—I'd all but forgotten it in the wake of everything that happened. Now, it pulses with a strange violet light.

The amulet, I realize.

Westlyn closes her eyes and tosses her head back, her hair suddenly whipping around her face. I watch in stunned silence as electric bolts of raw power spark up from the ground around her like reverse lightning, then spin, encircling her in a whirlpool of light.

The air crackles with dark magic. Every hair on my body stands at attention.

"Westlyn," I say softly, raising my hands as I approach her. "It's all right, love. You're safe."

At the sound of my voice, she finally raises her head and

opens her eyes. She looks straight at me—straight through me. I hardly recognize her.

Tiny bolts of light flicker across her skin.

Fae runes, I realize. Hundreds of them. Impossibly tiny, but unmistakable.

"He will punish you for this," she says cooly, her voice as eerie as the runes. "This is *not* what he demands of you."

At first I think she's speaking to me, but then I sense a presence behind me.

Eloise.

"You'll come to your senses sooner than you realize, girl," she spits. "And when you do, I won't be able to help you. Don't say I didn't warn you."

I whip around, claws out, but she's already vanishing into the shadows.

One more heartbeat, and the woman is gone.

The violet light fades, and soon, that too is gone.

All that remains is Westlyn, pale and trembling, staring off into the distance as if she doesn't even know who she is.

CHAPTER EIGHT

DRAEGAN

Westlyn sways on her feet.

I catch her before she falls, sweeping her into my arms and hauling her against my chest. The runes are gone. No trace of magic remains on her skin.

Only the scent of it, like the air before a wild summer storm.

"Westlyn," I whisper. "Talk to me. Tell me you're all right. Tell me you can hear me."

Still clutching that damn briefcase, she finally reaches up to touch my cheek with her free hand. Through a faint smile, she says softly, "I knew you'd save me."

It's an effort not to fall to my knees in relief.

"Of course I saved you." I brush the hair from her eyes and force a grin, hoping it hides my lingering fear. "I've got an unbroken record now. Couldn't very well ruin my streak."

She laughs, but I can tell it's a struggle for her to keep her eyes open. "I... I was so worried about you, Draegan. When I first came to, I couldn't find you, and I thought—"

"Shh. It's over now. I'm here, you're safe, the mages are dead."

"Eloise?"

"She... slipped away. But we'll find her, love. I promise."

"She saw you, though. Goddess, Draegan. She saw your true form. She knows you're a gargoyle."

"It was always a risk. Honestly, I'm surprised it hasn't happened sooner."

"But what if—"

"Wait... Do you hear that?"

"The breeze?"

"No, it sounds more like—"

The realization slams into me with shocking clarity. The hiss and whoosh of a flame catching. Spreading.

There's no time to run. No time to even think. I drop to my knees and wrap her in my wings, turning to stone just as the car bursts into flames right behind us, exploding in an epic wall of fire.

If I thought time stood still in the forest for those brief minutes when I couldn't find her, that was nothing compared to this.

It's an age. A fucking *eternity* before I finally feel the flames recede.

I shift back into my gargoyle form, my wings trembling.

She's gone still in my arms. Is she breathing? Was she burned before I had a chance to fully turn to stone?

My throat closes around a knot of fear so intense, I'm not sure I'll ever breathe again.

Fuck.

Forcing myself to take a breath, I slowly roll back my wings and glance down at the soft, silent form curled against my chest.

Her cheeks are smudged with dirt and soot, her hair a tangled mess.

But when she blinks up at me and smiles, I know she's still with me. Still here. Still Westlyn Avery, despite everything she's been through tonight.

"Okay, seriously?" She coughs through another faint smile. "Now I'm starting to think you've got a hero complex."

"When it comes to keeping you alive? Absolutely." Drawing her closer, I press my lips to the crown of her head. "Bloody hell, woman," I mutter. "I thought you were... You nearly gave me a heart attack."

"*I* gave *you* a heart attack?" she teases. "You're the one who blew up your own car just so you'd have another excuse to save me."

I laugh and shake my head at her, the lightness in her eyes doing more to heal my wounds than the dark fae magic that's kept me alive for centuries.

But then she notices the burns on my arms. The smoldering holes near the tips of my wings. I've only just begun to feel them myself—the fire must've hit me before I fully solidified.

"Draegan. You... you're hurt."

"I'll be fine. I'll heal in minutes."

"But—"

"I'm fine. You, on the other hand." My gaze sweeps her face, a hand sliding over her head. "You gave me quite a scare. Those runes... Did you call them up intentionally? And who did you mean when you told Eloise he would punish her?"

I have a dozen more questions for her, but I swallow them all the moment I see the utter confusion knitting her brow.

"What runes?" she asks. "*Punish*? I don't... Draegan. What on earth are you talking about?"

Damn it. It sounds like the same sort of thing that happened at the Ryker plant. Something just... overtook her. And then it was gone, leaving her with no memory of the incident.

"It's... nothing." I force another smile. "Just more shadow mage trickery."

"Draegan, you're starting to freak me out."

"We'll talk tomorrow—I promise. Right now, I just need to get you home."

"What about the—"

"Now what in the flaming, fucking, *bleeding* arseholes happened here?" a familiar voice demands.

Jude.

Relieved and more than grateful for the presence of one of our own, I turn to see him and Augustine land in the street before us, wings fluttering as they tuck them in close and take in the scene.

The moment they notice Westlyn in my arms, they're both on us, Augustine stroking her hair, Jude damn near vibrating with sudden rage.

"Explain," Jude demands.

"There was an accident," Westlyn says. "Sort of."

"Are you hurt?" he asks her, his voice softening.

"No. Just completely freaked out."

"You've never been in an accident," he says to me. "Not once since the bloody automobile was invented. We couldn't reach you for hours. What the *hell* is going on?"

"Wasn't an accident," I say, fighting to keep my voice even. "Shadow mages. Eloise tried to take Westlyn."

Jude's eyes widen. "But she *didn't* take her, because you killed her. Right?" He grips the tip of my wing. "Tell me you gutted that worthless cunt, or—"

"We were outnumbered. I took down four mages, but she escaped, and—Jude! Where the fuck are you going?"

He's already turning toward the woods, the crazy bastard.

"She can't have gone far," he says.

"Eloise is long gone by now," I say. "Shadow magic—they can basically teleport."

"Fuck." He shoves a hand through his dark hair, and for the first time tonight, I notice the dried blood on his hands.

Lovely.

"I thought you were helping Rook with research tonight," I say, more exhausted than angry at this point.

"We *were* helping him with research," Jude says. "Had to do a couple of in-person interviews."

Fucking Jude.

I don't even want to know. Not now. I've got too much to worry about with Westlyn at the moment.

"Is Rook with you?" I ask.

"He's back at the manor," Augustine says. "Apparently something went down with the Codex."

"Codex?" Westlyn's eyes widen. "What happened?"

"Whatever it is," I say, glaring at Augustine, "I'm sure Rook will fill us in later." Then, nodding toward the forest where I left the slaughtered mages, "You two... Deal with the bodies and search the other car—see if there's anything useful."

"What about your car?" Augustine asks. "Not that there's anything left to salvage."

"I'll call in a favor—get it towed out of here tonight without any questions. In the meantime, I need to get Westlyn back to Blackmoor and see to her injuries."

"I'm not injured," she murmurs in my arms, but her voice is growing faint, and dark circles bloom beneath her eyes.

"Humor me, love. Hero complex, remember?" I draw her into another tight embrace, more to calm myself than to calm her.

Bloody hell, I nearly lost her tonight—more than once. She could've died in my car. She could've been thrown from the wreckage. She could've been torn apart by those mages or kidnapped by Eloise or fried by whatever dark fae magic seems to have its claws in her soul, and *all* of those things would've been my fault.

I think of her fiery gaze in the car tonight, moments before the crash.

I think of her quiet bravery in the bank, trying to make sense of a past that's been kept from her.

I think of everything that happened between us earlier—her smart mouth, her soft moans, her devious little tongue, the feel of her silky skin as I kissed that spot on the back of her neck and everything inside me wants to fucking *explode* with fury at the mere thought that those mages put their hands on her. That her stepmother came so close to stealing her away. That she could've been irreparably harmed...

I never should've brought her into the city. I was a fool to think I could keep her safe with my presence alone.

"Fine," she says softly, a yawn overtaking her. "Just try not to blow anything else up on the way home, okay? Your nightly quota of heroic acts is officially full."

"I promise," I whisper, though I'm not sure she even hears me. She's passed out in my arms, finally succumbing to the post-adrenaline, post-magic exhaustion. As gently as I can manage, I take the briefcase from her and reposition her in my arms for the flight home. We're not far, but I'm not taking any more chances tonight.

Then, turning back to Jude and Augustine with a final nod, I say only, "Come *straight* home when you're done. And watch your fucking backs."

CHAPTER NINE

JUDE

"There's nothing I love more than making you wriggle for me, scarecrow. But in this particular endeavor, I must insist." I tighten my grip on Westlyn's bare foot and drag my gaze up the length of her shorts-and-T-shirt clad body, shooting her a scornful look. "Hold still or you'll make me smudge, and I'll have no choice but to tie you down and start over."

Stretched out on her back in Draegan's bed—yes, *Draegan's* bed, which I'm trying not to make a big deal about because sometimes you just have to be the bigger person—she grins at me and rolls her eyes. "Don't threaten *me* with a good time, mister."

I dip the nail polish brush back into the bottle for another drop of color. Mango Madness, this one's called. Like a sunrise for your toes, or so the nice girl at Sephora told me when I popped over to Kingston to get Westlyn a few treats earlier. "Draegan says you're in no condition to be tied down and ravaged, so don't give me any ideas."

She shoots me a dubious look. "Really? He said those exact words?"

"I'm paraphrasing, but—"

"Since when do you follow his orders, anyway?"

"Oh, I don't know. Since you nearly died the other night and I wasn't there to protect you? That's probably my best guess."

"So *dramatic*." She laughs and nudges me with her pretty toes, and I return to the task at hand, but I know she's still a bit out of sorts about the whole thing.

We *all* are.

Other than a few minor cuts and bruises, she escaped the ordeal without physical injury. But a few trips to the bathroom notwithstanding, she's basically been in bed for over thirty-six hours now. Alert and asking questions about what happened, trying to help us put some of the pieces together as well, but not keen to do much else. I was more than a little relieved when she woke up earlier tonight complaining about the state of her pedicure—that, at least, was something normal and mundane. Something I could help her with and bring a smile back to her pretty mouth.

Draegan filled us all in about her little lights-and-magic show on the road, not to mention the mysterious runes, but even after hearing his full report, she still can't remember it. She remembers accessing *some* sort of magic earlier that night—something that gave her a glimpse at her stepmother's crazy thoughts—but then it was gone, and she hasn't been able to call it up again since.

Which might be for the best. When it comes to her formerly nonexistent magic—not to mention the dark fae lineage that may be partially responsible for it—none of us have any idea what we're dealing with yet.

"Any news from Rook about the SSD card?" she asks now.

"Last I checked, he was still running it through some algorithms or code breakers or... I don't know, exactly. He tried to explain it to me, but to be perfectly honest, my eyes started glazing over about thirty seconds in, and the next thing I knew I was asleep on my feet and he was near about ready to bash me in the head with a book. But fear not. If there's anyone who can break into anything digital, it's our resident genius."

She nods, propping herself up a bit higher with the pillows so she can inspect my progress on her toes. "Any updates on the hit?"

"We didn't find anything of interest in the car that hit you, but Rook's contact at the DMV confirmed the registration—it's definitely one of the shadow mages who also attended your wedding. Based on the descriptions Draegan gave him, Rook pulled up some of the video footage from the cathedral and thinks he's got the other three arseholes identified as well. All Forsythe's guests, of course."

"Why am I not surprised? Goddess, they're an incestuous bunch."

"There's more." I bring her foot close to my lips and blow across her wet toes. "Assuming we've got the right blokes—all four mages are also long-time members of the Starlight Club."

"Starlight Club? Wait, the sex club the banker guy owns?"

"Indeed."

She bolts upright, making me lose my grip on her foot and smudge the polish on her baby toe. "So Kevin Klaiburn's a mage, too? That crusty fucker!"

"He's not a mage, but he's obviously connected to Forsythe and his flock. They're probably some of his best clients."

"Klaiburn sold us out! He must've contacted them as soon as Draegan gave him my father's name for the safe deposit box. It's like they knew about it all along and were just waiting for me to make my move so they could track me. Do you think my father set me up, leaving me that stuff at the bank?"

"I don't know, scarecrow. Anything's possible, but that one seems a bit of a stretch. If it was a setup, I think your father would've made it a bit easier for you to recall he'd left something for you at the bank rather than relying on you to piece together random clues from an old photograph and scant memories from your childhood."

She seems to relax a bit, and I pick up her foot to redo the smudged toe.

"It's possible the mages had other informants either

working at the branch or on the bank's security team," I say. "Or that Klaiburn just recognized the name Brian Avery and contacted Forsythe on that matter alone. But either way—yes. It's clear the mages knew you and Draegan were at the bank and when you left. The crash was planned."

"Which means they also knew where I was going. Right here." A nervous shudder rolls through her body.

"They can't reach us here, scarecrow. Rook's got everything locked down—you know that. The best they could do is set up shop on the land across the road and hope that you leave the property, which is obviously not happening."

She huffs out a sigh. "Guess this means there aren't any more road trips in my future."

"Tell you what, darling. Once we finish slaughtering all these mages and sending Zorakkov back to hell? I'll drive you anywhere you want to go. We'll take one of Draegan's cars—really get on his good side."

A faint laugh bubbles up, but it doesn't last. "What about the other guy?" she asks. "The car that left the scene? Was Rook able to get a match on the license plate?"

"He's awaiting confirmation on that one," I say. "Should know soon enough."

"He just got it." A shadow crosses the room, and Draegan looms in the doorway, crossing his arms over his chest. He shoots me a glare—probably worried about me getting Mango Madness all over his pristine white sheets—then says, "The other vehicle is registered to one Grant Reedsy. *Detective* Grant Reedsy."

CHAPTER TEN

JUDE

"Are you fucking shitting me?" I ask.

Westlyn's eyes widen. "The asshole who's been investigating you guys?"

"The one and only." Draegan crosses the room to join us by the bed. "Rook hacked into the cell tower relay system and determined Reedsy made a call about fifteen minutes before the crash, then another a few minutes after. He was most likely calling Eloise to report that you were en route, then again to confirm the crash had happened. Rook spotted the mage's car in traffic surveillance footage from the Lincoln Tunnel entrance out of Manhattan just after you and I passed through—there was only a single driver. Eloise and the others were likely already upstate, waiting nearby for the signal to make their move."

Westlyn leans back against the pillows, her turquoise eyes shining. "So much trouble. So much effort just to get to me. One witch. How could I be so important to their plans? Even if I *wanted* to help Eloise usher in the freaking apocalypse... How could she think I possibly have that much power?"

"We're still trying to figure that out," I say gently. Satisfied her toes are perfect, I cap the polish and set it on the bedside table. "Augs and I learned a few things about Hunter from Belinda Eckhardt, but unfortunately she offed herself before we could get her to talk about your role in all of this."

I tell West and Draegan about our adventures with Belinda and the Yankee Candle, filling them in on everything the good doctor spilled. The details, I mean, not the blood and tears. Figure they don't need the play-by-play on the latter. Besides, Drae's still riled up about the fact that we went after Nesterman against his orders, but if we hadn't? Well. That'd be two more fucking dickheads on the list of people still capable of hurting our girl, and fuck *those* odds.

"I get the sense Hunter's body might be failing," I continue. "She didn't say it outright—said her recent visits were out of concern for him after West ditched his arse at the altar. But we know that's a load of utter shite."

"Failing how?" she asks.

"I'm not sure exactly, but I have a feeling it's related to the demon binding. Seems like they were counting on you to help sustain his physical body during the possession, or help keep the demon inside him... I'm not exactly sure how it all works. But since you fled the scene, so to speak, the doctor had to give him more treatments. That's my best guess."

"So now I'm demonic superglue?" She rolls her eyes again. "Awesome. Add it to my resume."

I squeeze her ankle, careful not to mess up the toes. "The good news is, without his witch augmenter *or* in-house physician, Hunter is now free to rot, burn, and fuck off into the proverbial sunset."

"I take it you didn't leave any witnesses?" she asks, but there's no judgment there. Just a wry little smile that reminds me once again what a fucking gem she is.

"Darling. When do I *ever* leave witnesses?" I close my eyes, a grin stretching across my face as I recall the carnage Augs and I left behind in that awful house.

"Dare I ask what you're smiling at now?" Draegan says.

"Oh, just imagining the masterpiece I'm going to make from Belinda's ribs."

His sigh is heavy and all-encompassing. "For fuck's sake, Jude."

I open my eyes and meet his incredulous—and entirely predictable—glare. "Draegan. Did you honestly think I'd come home empty-handed after all that hard work? No, thank you. I got me some *nice* souvenirs."

"Of course you did."

"Huff and puff all you want, Negative Nelly, but I'll be expecting a full apology when you're out on the porch with a hot toddy next week, enjoying the soothing sounds of our new wind chimes. They're supposed to be good for your blood pressure—did you know that?"

"Not as good as time away from you." He shakes his head, then turns to Westlyn, his irritation melting into something that almost looks like affection. "Feeling better, then? You look good. I mean... That is to say, your color is... nice."

"I'm fine, Daddy Drae." Her tone is casual, her smile bright, but those eyes hold an unmistakable spark of mischief. Lifting her foot off the bed, exposing a particularly juicy section of her thigh, she says, "Jude gave me a pedicure. Do you like it?"

Draegan's eyes blaze in return, his hands curling into fists at his side.

I'm no couples therapist, but I'm ninety-nine percent sure they fucked the other night. Not that either of them will admit it to me, of course. I'm about to ask them, just to break the tense silence, but then Draegan clears his throat and says, "It's... lovely. You... continue to rest up. Let me know if you need anything."

With that, he turns on his heel, about to bolt out of his own bedroom like he's just heard the postman deliver the latest Architectural Digest, but Augs shows up with a massive tray loaded up with all of Westlyn's favorites. Lucinda and Huxley follow him in.

Drae halts his speedy exit, if only to share some of his special brand of sunshine with Auggie. "What's all this?" he demands, gesturing irritably at the birds. "I hope you cleaned their feet."

"This," Auggie says, smoothly side-stepping him, "is for Westlyn. Room service with a smile, and a couple of friends along for the ride."

"Night breakfast in bed, huh?" Westlyn grins and rubs her hands together. "Careful, boys. A witch could get used to this."

"Would that be so bad?" Augs leans down to set the tray beside her and kisses her forehead, the birds hopping up beside them, and the whole scene is just downright cozy, if you ask me.

But Draegan? Not exactly the cozy type. He just crosses his arms over his chest and glares at us like he's about to pop off.

"Jude," he says abruptly. "Augustine. Maybe we should let Miss Avery get some rest. I'm quite sure she could use it after her ordeal, and—"

"I'm quite sure *she* can speak for herself," Westlyn says, giving Drae a playful roll of her eyes. "But I'm fine. Just a little stiff. Nothing a good meal and some quality time with my gargoyles won't fix."

"Define... quality." Auggie sits beside her and leans in close, lips grazing her ear. "Because I'm fairly certain I can provide some top-tier—"

"*Augustine*." Draegan, again with the glaring.

"*Draegan*," the three of us tease in return. Then Westlyn pops a strawberry into her mouth and says to him with an adorable shrug, "You're welcome to join us, Daddy Drae. Plenty of room for more on this big bed of yours."

Heat creeps into his haughty face, though it's hard to tell if he's angry or turned on. "Thank you, but I certainly don't need an invitation to my own bed. And if you don't mind, kindly escort the birds away from the pillow shams. They're... Anyway, I have... things. Things to do. To see to. Many, many things."

"Don't let us hold you up," I say, hopping up onto the bed on Westlyn's other side. "Oh, don't worry. I'll be mindful of the pillow shams."

Casting a final icy glower at me and Augs, Draegan finally leaves us in peace.

"Sooo." Auggie nudges her thigh with his knee. "How long have you and Drae been fucking?"

Her eyes widen, then she plucks another big, juicy strawberry from the bowl and shoves it into Auggie's mouth.

"No more talking," she says. "I'm eating."

I can't help but grin. *Suspicions confirmed.*

CHAPTER ELEVEN

JUDE

Westlyn practically inhales her breakfast, sparing only a few meager bites for Lucinda and Huxley and refusing to share anything at *all* with her gargoyles—a thing neither Auggie nor I complain about. Her appetite is finally back—and with a vengeance. That can only be a good sign.

When she finally downs the last of her latte, and Auggie's sure she won't stab his claw with a fork for taking away the scraps too soon, he removes her tray and brings it back to the kitchen. The birds trail after him, probably hoping he'll drop one of the few remaining crumbs.

Westlyn and I are, for the moment, alone.

Moonlight shines down on us through Drae's windows, and I look at her profile, her cheeks pink, her tousled hair spilling in waves over her shoulders, and my chest tightens.

To think she almost slipped away from us. That if Drae

and the birds hadn't gotten to her when they did, Eloise might've taken her from us...

Fury boils up inside me, tempered only by what I feel for her.

She leans back against the pillows again and wriggles her toes, admiring the polish. Then, turning to me with a smile that melts my heart, she says, "I never thought I'd see the day Jude Hendrix gave me the best pedicure I've ever had." She glances down at her toes again. "Just look at that color. That shine. Seriously, Jude. I think you missed your true calling."

"Westlyn." My voice is barely a whisper, my throat knotted with emotion. I cradle her face in my hands, my gaze sweeping down to her mouth, then back to her eyes.

Three words. Three small, single-syllable words. They rise inside me now, chasing off the last of my anger about her plight.

For fifteen hundred years, I've been utterly dead inside, my heart so frigid I was certain I'd forgotten those words, forgotten how to say them, forgotten what they even meant. Yet looking at her now, holding her face in my hands, feeling her warm breath on my skin, I know I haven't forgotten. They've been here all along, tucked away inside me behind all the bitterness and rage and regret, quietly waiting for the moment when this soft, feisty, crazy, beautiful witch crossed my path.

Waiting for *this* moment.

And now that it's here, those words well up, threatening to burst me open like a ripe melon.

She gazes at me intensely, her eyes wide. "Oh no. *Westlyn?* The real name again. Whatever it is, just tell me, Jude. If I have to hear any more bad news, I'd rather get it all at once. Rip off the—"

"*Westlyn,*" I say again. "I love you. *That's* what it is." I swallow the lump lodged in my throat and try again, clear and sure this time. "I'm in love with you. So you're damn bloody right I'm giving you the best pedicure you've ever had, along with the best foot massages, the best kisses, the best... the best of anything you desire. Hell, woman. You already have my heart. Whatever else you want? Name it and I'll make it so."

Westlyn's worried frown stretches into a smile, her eyes shining.

"Anything?" she whispers.

"Anything."

"The bones of my enemies?"

Fuck. It lights me up inside, the way she's grinning about that, the little psycho. "Every last one of them, if that's what it takes to keep that light dancing in your eyes."

"Jude." She closes her eyes, placing her hands over mine. A single tear slides down her cheek, but she's still smiling. In a soft, shy voice, she says, "I'm... I'm pretty sure I'm in love with you, too."

I can't help the laugh that explodes out of me. "Pretty sure?" I tease. "*Pretty* sure? I confess my deepest feelings, bare my soul, offer you the bones of your enemies—which, by the way, I've already proven I can deliver—and *that's* the response I get?"

I tackle her on the bed, climbing on top of her and ravishing her with kisses—her cheeks, her jaw, her neck. She giggles beneath me, laughing and squirming until she finally admits the truth.

"I'm sure!" she squeals. "I'm positive!"

"Positive about *what?*" I demand, my mouth hovering just a hair's breadth from hers.

Her smile fades, her eyes turning serious. She brings her palm up to my cheek, and I lean into her soft touch.

"I'm positive I love you, Jude Hendrix," she whispers.

I brush a kiss to her lips, then bring my mouth to her ear. "Say it again, darling."

She threads her fingers into my hair, then up around my horns. "I love you, Jude Hendrix."

I can't hold back another moment. I crash into her, claiming her mouth in a possessive kiss, my hands sliding up her shirt, palms skimming over her nipples. She moans into my mouth and arches against me, tightening her grip on my horns, stroking them, and... *fuck*, she feels so good. Tastes so good. I'm hard in an instant, three seconds from tearing off yet *another* set of shorts and panties—

"Draegan's gone," Auggie says, barging back into the room. "Left for a meeting with—oh. Sorry. Am I interrupting?"

"Yes," I growl, at the same time Westlyn says, "Not if you're naked."

I shake my head and give her neck a playful bite. Then, rolling off her to glance at Auggie, "What meeting?"

"A new building inspector downtown—something about the hotel acquisition. Said he wasn't sure how long it would take, but we shouldn't wait up."

"That's it?" I ask.

"Well, he also wanted me to convey the message that he'd personally clip our wings if either of us touched Westlyn—and I quote—in any depraved or salacious manner detrimental to her recovery."

"What if my so-called recovery requires being touched in a salacious manner?" She grins, another devious sparkle lighting up her eyes. "If it's what I *need*, and my gargoyles refuse to touch me, I'll have no choice but to take matters into my own hands."

I exchange a look with Augs, and we both laugh. "Is that supposed to be a threat, darling?"

"You tell me," she says with a shrug. Then she closes her eyes, one hand sliding up the front of her T-shirt, the other slipping beneath the waistband of her shorts, her mouth parting on a soft moan as her hand begins to work in slow circles...

Fucking. Hell.

I try to watch her, to see it all the way through, but I can't go another moment without touching her, and judging from the massive cock tenting his loincloth, I'm pretty sure Auggie feels the same way.

I strip off my loincloth, grab her hands, and roll back on top of her, shoving my thigh between hers, grinding it against her wet heat.

"Jude," she breathes. "You'll... you'll mess up my pedicure."

"I'll give you another one." I wrap a hand around her throat, trailing another path of blazing hot kisses to her ear. In a dark whisper, I say, "You're a naughty little thing, darling, teasing me and Auggie like that. I don't give a fuck about your pretty toenails now, and you've only yourself to blame. All I care about now is stuffing your dirty mouth with my cock while Auggie rails you from behind until all three of us are coming so fucking hard, we break the bed. Unless, of course, you think such depravity would be detrimental to your recovery?"

"No, Jude." Westlyn smiles, already wriggling out of her clothing. "I'm pretty sure such depravity would just about cure me."

CHAPTER TWELVE

AUGUSTINE

Never one to stand on ceremony, I don't wait for a formal invitation.

One look into my witchling's hungry eyes, and I'm already getting naked and climbing into that bed.

Draegan's bed, I remind myself.

"The old man's gonna *love* this." I laugh, sliding in behind her and tossing his precious pillows to the floor.

"It's for a good cause." Westlyn rises to her knees, pushing Jude onto his back and settling herself between his thighs. "He wants me to recover, right?"

I nod. "Oh, absolutely. Above *all* else—he made that perfectly clear."

"See? You guys are actually following orders for change. He'll be thrilled."

"Not as thrilled as we are, trust me." I wrap my hands around her hips, positioning myself for a perfect view of her backside, dark waves tumbling down her back as she leans forward, slowly sliding her hands up Jude's muscular thighs, his cock bobbing beneath her mouth.

She doesn't take it, though. Not yet. Just drags her tongue along the shaft, then blows a soft breath over the tip, making him shudder.

It's an epic tease, because then she's rising up on her knees again, reaching behind her head to grip my horns as I gather her hair in my fist and kiss the back of her neck.

Touching her again, holding her, breathing in her scent... Fuck, it's the only thing that can chase away all the horrors of the other night—the filth of that house, the blood and gore, the fire, the crash. I would live through it a thousand times over if it meant I could come home to this every night. Home to her.

Tracing delicate swirls with my tongue, I drag my mouth from one shoulder to the other, then back up her neck, her jaw, finally settling near her ear, sucking her soft lobe between my lips. She arches her back and breathes out a sigh of pure pleasure, and I curve my tail around, sliding it between her thighs and gently flicking her clit.

"Does that feel good, witchling?" I murmur, teasing her entrance with the tip, then giving her clit another tap.

"Yes," she whispers. "I love how you touch me."

I cup her breasts, tugging her nipples to stiff peaks. The scent of her desire flares, stirring my cock to painful attention, and suddenly I'm remembering the first night she came to us.

She was terrified and alone after fleeing the wedding, running away from everyone she ever knew. But there was something so fierce about her, too—an inner fire that refused to be dimmed.

I felt an inexplicable connection from the moment I saw her walking down the aisle. But somewhere along the path from that very first night, to her annoying lectures about food quality, to seeing her with her birds, to watching her learn to stand up for herself and speak her mind to someone as downright intimidating as Draegan, to helping her unravel the mysteries of her past... that initial connection blossomed into something so much deeper.

That first night? Hell yeah, I fantasized about her. About kissing her lush mouth, bending her over the counter, and taking her in all the hot, delicious ways she'd have me.

But I never would've thought we'd end up here. Not just the physical part, as amazing as that is.

But the other parts.

She just... she feels like one of us. She belongs here.

And the idea that anyone would *dare* try to take that away from us—to shatter this bond—fills me with an icy, dreadful darkness that could very well consume me and anyone in my path.

But no. They didn't take her. Draegan and the ravens made sure of that. Westlyn *herself* made sure of that, the little badass.

I bury my face in her hair, once again inhaling her scent,

her presence, drowning out my fears and centering myself in *this* moment, *this* feeling.

This indescribable pleasure.

Slowly, I guide her back down on her hands and knees, and she skims her palms up Jude's thighs again, pressing a soft kiss to the base of his cock, then working her way to the tip with a trail of featherlight kisses.

"You're bloody *killing* me, darling," Jude practically purrs, threading his hands into her hair and gripping it tight, but letting her set the pace.

Slow. Excruciating.

Fucking perfect.

I lean back on my knees, fisting my cock and enjoying the show as she dips her head and takes him partway into her mouth.

They both moan at the contact, and I imagine her hot little tongue swirling around his flesh, her lips gliding over him, her warm breath tickling his skin.

"You like being shared, don't you?" I say softly, and she lets out another moan of pleasure. "Maybe we should call Rook."

She drags her head up, releasing Jude's cock just long enough to say, "Rook's busy working."

But I can tell from the breathiness in her tone, from the surge of desire in her scent... West would love nothing more than having her bookish gargoyle join the party.

I trace the tips of my claws lightly across the soft globes of her ass and down the backs of her thighs, making her shudder. "I'm pretty sure we could convince the illustrious president of the World's Sexiest Nerds club to take a study break. All in the name of your recovery, of course."

She and Jude both go still beneath me, silent, and for a minute I worry I've pushed her too far.

But then...

"Actually..." She turns to look at me over her shoulder, a devious smile cresting on her face. "I've got a better idea, if you guys are game?"

Fifteen minutes later, I've got the lighting arranged perfectly and my favorite high definition video camera set up on the tripod, perfectly positioned to capture absolutely *everything*.

Award-winning cinematography right here, folks. Yes, I'm already writing the Academy acceptance speech in my mind.

"Oy." Jude snaps his fingers and points at the camera. Still sprawled out with his head at the end of the bed with Westlyn kneeling between his legs, he says, "Make sure you angle that thing to get my good side, Augs."

"You don't have a good side," I remind him, hitting the record button.

"Be serious, now. It's my first on-camera performance with full frontal, and Rook's a tough critic. I'm keen to make a good impression."

Westlyn cracks up. "I can't speak for the cameraman or the critics, but I know *exactly* where your good side is, Jude Hendrix." Without giving him a chance to respond, she leans forward again, gripping the base of his massive cock, swallowing half his hard length in a single thrust.

After all her slow and careful teasing, the sudden deep-throat clearly surprises him, and he growls and bucks his hips, unable to keep himself from fucking deeper into that hot little mouth.

West takes it like a champ, bobbing her head to pick up the pace, then pulling back, her cheeks hollowing as she sucks him hard.

"Bloody fucking *hell*, woman," he grinds out. "That's... *fuck*. You're... you're just... bloody perfect."

Peering at the camera's viewing screen, I watch the black-and-silver waves of her hair undulate with the motions of her head, Jude's claws tightening against her scalp as she licks and sucks, her nails scraping down his thighs, and fuck this angling-for-the-perfect-shot bullshit.

I need to be in that fucking bed. Now.

Trusting the camera to do its job, I climb back in behind her, hauling her up by the hips and positioning myself between her thighs, spreading her wide. She's already glistening with desire, more than ready to take me in, but it's not time for me to fuck her just yet.

Not with my cock, anyway.

First, I want a taste.

Keeping a firm grip on her thighs, I lower my mouth to

her exposed flesh and give her a long, languid lick, making her gasp around a mouth full of Jude's cock.

A low growl vibrates through my chest. The taste of her... *Fuck*. I meant what I told her the other night. I want my first meal of every fucking night to be *this*. Her. For the rest of my cursed existence.

One more long lick, and then I'm picking up the pace, teasing her, tempting her, driving her wild. We've spent enough time together that I know exactly what she likes, how hard, how fast, how deep, and it's not long before I've got her writhing for me. I swirl my tongue around her clit, then draw back, blowing a hot breath over her flesh before finally spearing her, sucking her, burying my whole fucking face in her soft, wet heat until I'm absolutely *feasting* on her.

Ripples of pleasure course through her thighs, her muscles tensing beneath my grip, her ass grinding back to meet every thrust of my tongue, again and again and again until...

A strangled cry erupts from deep inside her, and she comes around my tongue with a shudder that rockets throughout her entire body and straight into mine. My lips, my tongue, my chest, right down to my aching balls.

Rising up on my knees again, I grab my cock and drag it through her wetness, seconds from burying myself to the hilt with a deep, delicious thrust...

A sudden movement in the doorway stops me cold.

Fuck. We're busted.

I tense, glancing up to meet our intruder's gaze.

But it *isn't* Draegan coming home early to scold us for messing up his fine linens and interfering with her "recovery."

It's Rook.

He briefly meets my eyes, then scans the room, taking in the whole scene. A soft breath hisses from his lips, and every muscle in his body goes rigid.

But the look in his eyes is pure, liquid fire.

Westlyn lifts her head, and I can already picture the grin sliding across her pretty, swollen mouth.

"Good evening, professor," she says, her voice low and sultry. "Funny—I was *just* thinking about you."

CHAPTER THIRTEEN

ROOK

That ripe, red mouth. That sexy-as-sin voice. The sweet blush of pleasure and the sight of Auggie's glistening chin and Jude's cock twitching near her lips and the raw, uncut scent of her desire invading my senses...

All of it conspires to steal the breath from my lungs.

And then I see the camera.

Fuck...

I can't form words. Can't move. All I can do is hold my breath and blink at them... and hope like hell I don't die of a massive heart attack. It would be a first for an immortal, but at this point? It wouldn't surprise me. My heart feels like it's about two more beats from exploding right out of my chest.

The smile on West's face widens, and she stretches out her hand, reaching across the softly lit space to beckon me closer.

Somehow, I force my feet to move. One awkward step, then two. A few more, and I stop a couple of feet from the end of the bed, not daring to get any closer.

"Were your ears ringing?" she asks, her eyes dancing with light and lust—a combination I can't help but love.

Beneath her, Jude grits his teeth and groans at the loss of contact, his hips rocking, still seeking the return of her hot, wet mouth.

I reach out and run a finger over the top of the camera, noticing the blinking red recording light. "Are you... Are you filming this for me?"

Damn. The very thought of it is so fucking sexy, so erotic it sends another jolt of electricity through me.

"Well, we *were* filming it for you," she says. "But now that you're here, you can join us for the live demo."

I nod, but don't say another word. Don't move. Once again, I'm frozen in place, my heart kicking into high gear.

"Oh, all right." She lets out a teasing huff. "If you'd really rather watch from the sidelines, Professor Peepshow, be my guest. But feel free to change your mind at *any* time."

I know she means it. The invitation is clear in her voice, in the desirous way she's still looking at me, and I'm so, *so* close to finally giving in, but...

No. I'm not ready for this. For her. For the feel of her mouth on my flesh, her hair in my hands, her teeth grazing my shoulder to muffle her cries of passion as I bury myself deep.

And as much as she claims to want me, she's not ready

for this, either. For all the things I want to do to her. For all the filthy, beautiful ways I want to see her *completely* unravel for me.

Heat blooms in my chest at the thought.

That night will come soon enough.

But for now?

I finally relax, and a return smile curves my lips. As long as she and the others are okay with an audience, these little spy games will satisfy me *just* fine.

Already knowing my answer, West shrugs and blows me a flirty little kiss, then finally turns her attention back to Jude. The gargoyle growls with unrestrained pleasure as she lowers her mouth to his cock and licks the tip, gently squeezing his balls.

He looks like he's about to burst. Auggie, too, kneeling behind her and slowly dragging his cock along her backside, his wings unfurled, his tail curved around the front of her thigh to brush against her clit, and I can't help but wonder how long the three of them have been at it.

"Please," I finally manage. "Carry on. I'll just... right." I lean back against the wall, my eyes locked on the scene, a pulse of desire throbbing in my cock as they pick up where they left off.

And then, I do what I do best.

Watch.

With a soft grunt, Auggie tightens his grip on her hips and positions his cock at her entrance, giving her a smooth, slow thrust and another stroke of that tail that has her moaning and arching back to meet him, her pretty turquoise eyes fluttering closed. Her head dips low again, hair falling in front of her face as she takes Jude deeper into her mouth, into her throat, alternating between massaging his balls and stroking the base of his cock with a tight fist.

Jude clutches the sheets at his side, squeezing until his knuckles turn white, his claws shredding the fabric, his body covered in a thin sheen of sweat as West continues to work her seductive charms. Behind her, it's not long before Auggie's measured thrusts pick up the pace, then turn into a feverish pounding, his thighs slapping against hers, the wet, greedy sounds of her slick pussy colliding with the increasingly sloppy sounds of Jude's cock fucking her mouth —a symphony of utter debauchery that makes my own balls heavy with the need to unload.

My breath comes in short, staccato bursts, my skin hot, my mouth watering at the sight.

Watching Auggie and West on the library security video was mind-blowing enough. But this? Live action, every sound, every scent, every perfect visual seared in my memory?

There are no fucking words.

And West...

Oh, how I want her. So desperately I can already taste the sweetness of her kiss, feel the silk of her hair sliding through my fingers as I guide her head between *my* thighs, her soft tongue darting out to lick *my* aching cock, her wet pussy hungry for *me*, and... *Fuck*... it's all about to send me into a fucking tailspin.

I don't know how Jude and Auggie do it. How they can last even five minutes inside her when I'm about to lose it just from watching. Imagining. *Fantasizing*.

Her mouth still full of Jude's thick cock, West glances up at me through dark lashes, her cheeks pink. I hold her gaze as I bring my tail up beneath my loincloth, the end wrapping around my stone-hard cock. The sensation makes me twitch. I'm so fucking over-sensitive, so desperate for contact, one stroke has me feeling like I'm about to burst into flames.

"That's it, Rook," Auggie says, his voice raspy. "Fuck yourself. Show our little witchling what the sight of her on her knees for us does to you."

West is still watching me with those big, turquoise eyes, and Jude is practically growling, and Auggie's fucking her harder and faster, her perfect breasts bouncing with every thrust, and I don't even remember making the decision to obey him. One minute I'm watching them, fantasizing about her mouth and her hands and the taste of her dark pink nipples, and the next I've got my tail wrapped tighter around my cock, my gaze never leaving hers as I jerk myself off in time with Auggie's punishing thrusts.

"That's it, darling," Jude pants. "Suck it. Harder. Yeah, just like... *Fuck*, I'm gonna come down your perfect fucking throat. Are you ready for me?"

She groans and slides down his shaft, fighting past her

gag reflex to take him as far as she possibly can. Jude grabs her hair and holds her in place, his abs tightening, his hips bucking, and once again I feel her silky waves against my palms as if *I'm* the one guiding her over my cock, ready to claim that mouth.

"Take it," Auggie says, fucking her harder as his tail rubs her clit. "Make your gargoyles come for you, witchling." Then, his eyes flicking up to catch my gaze, "All *three* of your gargoyles."

She moans in response, and Jude roars, his whole body shuddering as he just fucking unloads. Auggie's wings ripple behind him, the corded muscles of his arms and shoulders tightening as he comes inside her with a dark growl. A fresh blush spreads across her bare skin, and then West arches backward, Jude's cock slipping from between her lips as she catches the wave of her own building release, Auggie's tail fucking her clit faster, pushing her to the very edge and right fucking over it.

My tail tightens around my cock, my strokes slowing, then speeding up again, faster, faster still, one hand sliding over the crown and—

"*Fuck*," I groan, and West cries out for the goddess, and I come hot and hard, shuddering with the rest of them as the intensity of the shared release fully overtakes us.

When the sounds of pleasure finally subside and I'm able to catch my breath again, I look up to see Westlyn lying on top of Jude, Auggie stretched out behind them. Both of the gargoyles watch her with wide, awe-stricken gazes.

Not only because of the ecstasy she just shared with them. With all of us.

It's her skin.

She's glowing.

Not just with the moonlight shimmering through the windows, but with some deep, inner magic that illuminates her entire being, head to toe.

I turn off the camera. Turn off the extra lighting.

It only makes her glow brighter.

She looks like some kind of dark angel, beautiful and terrifying. Breathtaking.

"So, this is new," she says with a laugh, holding up her hands and inspecting the strange light. "Completely freaky, but hey, bright side? At least it's not dark fae runes."

She laughs again, breaking the momentary spell, and the glow finally fades away.

"You okay?" I ask softly.

"Oh, I'm more than okay, Professor." She rolls onto her back, her cheeks flushed, her eyes clear. "Gargoyle double team? With live audience participation, besides? Best medicine a girl could ask for."

Jude sits up and pulls her into his lap, ravishing her with a series of kisses on her neck and shoulder. "Even Draegan would be quite pleased with your progress."

At the mention of Drae, some of the light dims from her eyes, but she keeps her smile in place. "Anyway, I'm *starving*. Let's say we shower and take a snack break. Oh, and we should probably change these sheets. They're covered in nail polish. Um. Among other things."

The three of them roll out of bed, Jude and Auggie still semi-hard at the sight of her bare flesh. I'm not fairing much better, truth be told.

But she's right. We need showers. We need food.

And then, as much as I hate to rain on a perfectly good naked picnic... We need to get back to work.

Jude and Auggie head out first, but West lingers in the doorway, holding out her hand for me.

It's another invitation, and this time I accept, pulling her into an embrace, my wings curling around her protectively. "You're fucking *beautiful*, Wild West. I could watch you every night, with or without the full accompaniment."

"Are you... okay?" she asks, gazing up at me with a tentative hope in her eyes. "I'm guessing you came up here for a reason *not* related to our little... ménage à gargoyle."

"Your guess is correct." I push my glasses back up my nose. "But I'll be the first to admit... As much as I would've loved the video, I'm *very* glad I didn't miss the live show."

At my admission, her smile brightens. "I'm glad, too." She stretches up on her toes, fingers curling over my shoulders. "What did you come to tell us, anyway? Were you able to crack the encryption?"

"Not yet. Whoever left it for you wanted it to be kept

safe from prying eyes, but that's a good thing. Makes our job a bit harder, but I've never met a password I couldn't eventually crack."

She nods, her smile falling just a bit.

Tucking a finger under her chin, I say, "I came up here to tell you I found some more demon intel in one of the occult journals we nabbed from Forsythe's library."

"Yeah?"

"You up for hitting the books with me tonight? The last couple nights haven't been the same without my research assistant. I've missed your... input."

West laughs. "Input? Is that what we're calling it?"

"It's true. Your observations and analyses have been spot-on. And your questions always lead *me* to dig deeper, and that's an important quality in any—"

"Rook?" She presses a finger to my lips, silencing me. "It's totally okay if you missed my sparkling personality and great ass, too. I know I missed yours."

"Oh! Fishing for compliments, are we?" Laughing, I slide my hands down to cup the aforementioned great ass, lifting her up and wrapping her thighs around my hips. She's still naked, heat radiating from her core, her skin slick against my stomach. My cock twitches, and I sigh, my mind already replaying her soft moans, her fluttering lashes, the blush on her cheeks as she came for us tonight.

In a low voice, I say, "I think even a casual observer untrained in the methods of scientific inquiry would know I missed more than your academic input, Wild West."

She beams at me. "Can I tell you a secret?"

"You know I love secrets."

"I'm still thinking about kissing you, Professor."

"What a coincidence," I say. "I'm *always* thinking about kissing you."

"Really?"

"Really."

"Well." She threads her hands into my hair, her touch warm and electric. "No time like the present, I always say."

"And *I* always say the best things come to those who wait." I draw her close, the mist of her warm breath tickling my lips. "I've been waiting for you my entire immortal life, Westlyn Avery. And when I finally kiss you, you're *damn* well going to remember it for the rest of yours."

CHAPTER FOURTEEN

WESTLYN

After a quick shower with my new Sephora bath goodies from Jude, I meet the boys and my ravens in the kitchen for an epic snack break featuring a mountain of sliced fruit and veggies, apple-cinnamon scones, and my favorite—almond joy latte chasers. Refueled and refreshed, Auggie and Jude decide to head into Kingston on a food and supply run, leaving me and my naughty professor to hit the books.

I didn't realize how much I missed the library—I've only been away from it a couple of nights. But stepping inside the barn now feels like reuniting with a long-lost friend, and for a minute I just stand there in the middle of the main floor, eyes closed, breathing in the comforting scents of wood, leather binding, and old parchment.

"Goddess, I love this place," I whisper.

"Same." Rook tosses another log on the fire and stands

to dust off his hands. "I've come to appreciate it a hell of a lot more since the big storm, too."

"I still can't believe that happened."

I *wouldn't* have believed it, either—if Rook had simply told me the harrowing tale himself, I would've sworn he was trying to cheer me up with some half-baked story about books coming to life in the library. But he showed me the video on the security feeds. The entire thing was captured in detail—the crazy violet light, the sparks, the tornado.

And then everything returning to its place as if all those books just needed to stretch their spines and stir up a little mischief.

"Given the timing of it," he says now, shooting the currently silent Codex a wary glare, "I'm fairy certain it's connected to the magical surge you experienced after the crash."

"Which may or may not be connected to this mysterious protection amulet."

The amulet sits on the mantle—he was looking into its origins, along with all the other mysteries of my life—and I pick it up. Just like the first time, it warms and pulses at my touch, immediately synching with my heartbeat.

For the briefest instant, something stirs inside my chest. Ancient and faint, but powerful—just like that strange magic I tapped into in the forest.

It fades before I can really pin it down.

"Draegan was right about the amulet," Rook says. "It's definitely fae-made, and it's clearly attuned to you and you alone. From my preliminary searches, based on the shape and style, and the materials used, it's only about ten years old. And it's not dark-fae forged, but light fae."

"Light fae? What does that mean?"

"It means that whoever commissioned it for you wanted to protect you against the dark fae."

"Even though I've got dark fae ancestry?"

Rook practically snorts. "Our ancestors are often the ones we most need protecting from."

"Fair," I say with a laugh. But then the rest of his words click into place in my mind. "Wait... ten years? That would mean it couldn't have come from my mother. She died more than twenty years ago."

"Exactly."

"Who, then? My father?"

Rook shrugs. "We have no way of knowing. All evidence indicates that your father was the one who put it in the lockbox, and he wanted you to find it with the SSD card. He must've known it was meant for you, or there'd be no point in giving it to you at all—it's nothing but a pretty ornament in the hands of anyone but the person it was created for. But... that's all we know."

"Goddess. Just *once*, I'd like a solid answer on something instead of a million new questions."

"Me too, West. But I think we're getting closer. Check this out—it's what I wanted to tell you about Zorakkov."

Setting the amulet back on the mantle, I follow him to his worktable and take a seat beside him on the bench. His wing curves around me, and I lean in closer, taking comfort in his calm, stately presence.

Flipping through the old journal he mentioned, he stops at a page where he's made some notes in the margins, complete with colored tabs. I smile at his nerdy adorableness.

"Apparently, Zorakkov's been looking to hitch a ride topside for ages," he says. "He's got a long history of bargaining with the fae. According to the occult scholar who wrote this journal, the demon prince and the dark fae nobles would often trade favors in the form of hellbound human souls."

"What would the fae want with human souls?"

"Dark magic, most likely. Fae can use objects as well as creatures from hell—including the souls of the damned—to bind curses."

I gasp. "Holy shit, Rook. Like yours?"

"It's possible, yes. Though our curse is so strong and so old, it's likely they needed more than a damned soul to bind it."

A shiver snakes down my spine. "So what did Zorakkov get in return?"

"I'm not sure, specifically, but considering he wanted to fully manifest here, it must've had something to do with that. Maybe he thought he could travel here freely through the fae portals, or that the fae nobles could craft some sort of dark magic spell to bind him to a living vessel. When that didn't work out, it seems he turned his sights on the mages."

"And Hunter, and his little wifey augmenter." I blow out a breath. "You know, now that we're talking about this... *Shit*, Rook. The dark fae thing—I saw something about the dark fae in Eloise's thoughts the other night."

The fire pops, and his wing draws closer around my shoulders. "Tell me."

"I forgot about that particular detail because it was just a flash, and everything else was such a confusing mess, but there was definitely a dark fae male. The same one that's been making random appearances in my nightmares."

"You're sure?"

"Positive. And given the fact that Eloise is clearly in bed with Zorakkov and the shadow magic society, *and* she knows I've got dark fae blood in my lineage somewhere, I wouldn't be surprised if the two factions are working together."

"Everything seems to point that way," he says with a sigh.

"Demons and mages and dark fae... *Goddess*. Whatever end-of-the-world circle jerk they're all fantasizing about, I just wish they'd leave me the hell out of it. With all that firepower, why the hell do they need a lowly witch augmenter, anyway?"

Rook cups my chin and kisses my forehead, his touch as gentle as his smile. "I think we've established you're not just some lowly witch augmenter, West. We may not understand your magic yet, but it's clear you've got it. Maybe it's been bound, maybe it's something you'll age into later in life, maybe you just need different training to learn to recognize and tap into it... But whatever the case, it's special. *You're* special. Don't ever doubt that."

His words wrap around my heart, bolstering me, lifting me out of the muck of my own dark thoughts before they spiral.

"Thanks," I whisper, leaning my head on his shoulder.

We relocate to the sofa and get back to work in companionable silence, my feet tucked in his lap, his big hand massaging my arches as he skims back through the journal and I catch up on the notes he's taken during my brief absence.

Dark fae. Shadow mages. Zorakkov. Hunter. The Forsythes. The amulet. My lineage, my magic, my past... All of it's connected. There's no denying that now.

But how? To what end?

And where does the Codex fit in? Does it truly contain a dark fae spell of unmaking? Will that be enough to free the gargoyles from their curse?

And why did it seem to explode with magic the other night at the exact time I myself connected with some deep, mysterious power?

On a hunch, I rise from the sofa and grab my amulet. Holding it in my palm, I wrap my fingers around it and close my eyes, focusing on its warmth, on its shape and texture, on its unique energy. I feel it then—like an invisible thread spooling out from my heart, traveling across my chest and down my arm, wrapping itself around the amulet and connecting us. Truly connecting us.

"West," Rook whispers, and I open my eyes to find him staring at me with a wide gaze, his glasses pushed up against his horns, his mouth open like he can't believe his eyes.

CHAPTER FIFTEEN

WESTLYN

I'm glowing again, just like I did upstairs. Only now the light is more violet than silver, pulsing in time with my heartbeat.

"I think the amulet is allowing me to tap into my magic. Either because it enhances it or... I don't know. Maybe the magic needs to know I'm safe before it surfaces." I smile, my eyes shining with wonder that borders on giddiness. This is the first time I've ever intentionally tried to call up something magical, and actually experienced a response. "I'm not a dud."

Rook beams. "I tried to tell you."

"No, you don't understand. I'm not a dud, Rook. I've got magic—you're right about that. Which means I'm not an augmenter. I can't be! Augmenters have no magic of their own."

Rook gets to his feet, his eyes dancing with the light of a

new discovery. "I never even thought about that. You're right, West. You're absolutely right."

"Which means—"

"Zorakkov doesn't need you."

"At least, not as an augmenter." I close my eyes again, my thoughts racing too quickly to follow. Did Eloise and the Forsythes already know I've got my own magic? Does Zorakkov? Did they try to bind me to him for some other, yet-to-be revealed purpose?

Damn it. It's yet another puzzle piece unlocking yet another thousand questions, but this realization feels different. Bigger, somehow. Important.

Rook's right. We are getting closer. Step by step, question by question, answer by answer.

I can feel it.

"The Codex," I say, opening my eyes. "After the storm, it's been quiet ever since?"

"Not so much as a single spark."

Still holding the amulet, I carefully make my way toward the other table, not wanting to set off another storm. The Codex sits quietly in the center, silent and unassuming. But the closer I get, the more I can feel its energy—like another thread reaching out to me.

I reach out with my free hand, placing my palm gently against the front cover, trying to tell it with my mind that I mean no disrespect. That I only wish to learn. That I have no ill intentions for whatever secrets it may contain.

"Please open for me," I whisper. "Please grant me

permission to share in the knowledge of the sacred Cerridwen Witches who came before us."

I hold my breath. One beat. Two.

And the Codex finally responds, opening to the middle of the book with nothing more than a quiet rustling of pages.

"That's how it started the other night," Rook says softly, coming to stand behind me. "Only with slightly more fire and brimstone."

"I think the fire and brimstone is making an appearance in other ways." The skin on the back of my neck heats up suddenly, this time accompanied by a searing pain across my skull. I gasp, clutching the amulet tighter, but I don't back away.

"West. You okay?"

"Fine. It's just... that same feeling as before. Like something's trying to... to claw its way out." Gritting through the pain, I pull my hair forward and rub the back of my neck. "Can you see the rune?"

Rook leans in close, cursing under his breath.

"I take that as a yes?"

"Do you mind if I take a few pictures?" He pulls out his phone. "I sent copies of Auggie's original photos to my occult studies contact at NYU. Just closeups of the rune —nothing identifiable, of course. She's been digging through her material on fae runes looking for a match. I want her to see these, too—see if we can get some clearer shots."

"It's fine," I say, blowing out a breath as the pain slowly begins to fade.

When he's finished taking the pictures, I sit down before the book, eager to see what's inside. Turning it back to the first page, I glance up at Rook and smile. "No lightning, rain, or wind. I'll take that as a good sign."

Rook laughs, the relief clear in his eyes, too. "I don't know, West. They say it's the quiet ones you need to watch out for."

"Like you?"

"Exactly like me."

"You know, Rook. One of these days you're not going to be able to resist my charms, and you're just going to scoop me into your arms and plant a big, wet kiss right on my—"

"Focus, West," he says firmly, but when he takes a seat on the bench beside me, his eyes still hold a playful spark. "We've been waiting all this time to open it. Let's see what's under the hood, shall we?"

Rook can't read it.

Not a single word or verse.

Whenever he glances at the page, the letters and delicate sketches it contains flutter and swirl and spin before his eyes, making it impossible to decipher.

I see it, too. It's as if they're performing for us, a rare

and magical dance as beautiful and entrancing as it is infuriating.

But when I hold my amulet, take a deep breath, and touch my fingertips to its delicate pages, the words become still. Slowly, carefully, they reveal themselves to me and me alone.

It's another miracle, and the sight of those words clarifying before me brings tears to my eyes.

But just because I can read the individual letters and words doesn't mean I can make a damn bit of sense of them when they're all strung together.

It's written in English—or at least, it's presenting itself to me in English. But the writing is so archaic and awkward, stuffed with metaphors so complex and convoluted even Rook's eyes are crossing when I try to read them out loud.

After countless failed attempts, we've finally opened the mysterious Cerridwen Codex. But, as usual, we're trading one answer for a thousand more questions.

I blow out a breath, rising from the table and heading over to the fireplace. Pacing. Always pacing.

Never before have I felt so daunted.

But I also can't recall a time when I've felt so hopeful, either.

The professor and I have a *lot* of work ahead of us. It's going to take time for me to make my way through the text, transcribing it into a fresh document that Rook and his occult studies friend can eventually—*hopefully*—translate.

And that's assuming the Codex continues to cooperate.

But goddess, the fact that we even got this far tonight? It's just... It's indescribable.

Rook joins me before the fire, and when I meet his eyes, I can't help the smile that spreads across my face.

"The Cerridwen Codex," I whisper. "The freaking Cerridwen Codex!"

"It's like it was waiting for you, West. Just waiting for you to connect with your magic and figure out how to reach out to it in a way it would understand."

"How did this even happen?"

With a soft sigh, he takes my hand, lacing our fingers together and squeezing tight. "I keep asking myself the same thing."

He holds my gaze, his honey-brown eyes shining in the light of the fire, and I can't help but think he's no longer talking about the Codex or the magic we unlocked tonight.

Seconds pass like hours, and still, Rook doesn't look away.

He cups my face, his thumb brushing across my lips, unleashing a torrent of butterflies in my stomach. My breath hitches, and I stretch up on my toes, reaching up to run my fingertips along his lightly bearded jaw...

"I... I think we've done enough work for tonight," he says, capturing my wrist and pressing a sizzling but all-too-brief kiss to my palm.

"What? But we've only just opened the book! There's so much more to read and transcribe, and we still have to—"

"Hey. Tonight was a good night, West. An *amazing* night.

Trust me—we've earned a break." He tucks a lock of hair behind my ear, and I try not to shiver at his every touch. "Besides, if memory serves..." He leans in close, his eyes dancing with new mischief. "There's a new movie available. Something about two gargoyles and a very feisty, very sexy, *very* insatiable witch."

"Rook Van Doren." I crack up. "Are you inviting me on a date?"

"A private screening." He holds out his arm as if to escort me. "You interested?"

Those butterflies whip into another frenzy inside me, and I take the offered arm and grin. "I'll make the popcorn."

CHAPTER SIXTEEN

AUGUSTINE

"Taste this. I think it may need more salt." Cupping my lovely sous chef's chin, I tip the wooden spoon into her mouth, anxiously awaiting her assessment.

From her perch on the counter, West nods, licking the excess from her lips in a way that has me staring at her mouth like a sex-starved idiot, remembering the way Jude and I took her last night—an event she's taken to affectionately calling our "Ménage à Trois Miracle Cure with a Voyeurism Booster Shot."

"Not more salt," she says, bringing my attention back to the cooking. "I think it could use a bit of cumin, though, and maybe a pinch of chili powder? Just a little something to punch it up."

"Brilliant." I lean in for a kiss, lingering until the sauce begins bubbling on the stovetop.

After spending the early part of the evening in the

library with Rook working on transcribing the newly opened Codex, we decided Blackmoor Manor was overdue for a feast. She wanted to celebrate the big win—the Codex finally beginning to reveal its secrets. And I wanted to celebrate the fact that she's still with us. That she survived the car crash and attempted kidnapping. That I even have the luxury of her company and her kisses while making dinner tonight.

We decided on the menu together—a vegan twist on some old Italian favorites, featuring a vegetable-pumpkin lasagna with a light tomato-sage sauce, vegan caprese salad, and a series of appetizers. I've just started dicing the tomatoes for the bruschetta when Draegan returns from the city, heading straight for the pantry and his not-so-hidden stash of cognac.

"Rough night at the office, dear?" I ask.

Pouring himself a double and downing it hastily, he says, "Remind me to never get involved in another hotel renovation project in which compromising with the twats on the city council is a requirement."

"Noted."

After pouring a second drink, he finally glances over at Westlyn, who's been silent since his arrival. His eyes soften, but the tension between them is still uncomfortably thick.

"Are you... feeling well?" he asks.

She flashes a double thumbs-up and a too-bright smile. "Great! Augs and I are making dinner."

Draegan nods. "Is there... anything else you need?"

"He and Jude went food shopping last night, so I think we're all set."

"No, I was thinking in terms of your... I thought... pain medication? Or... bandages. Maybe extra pillows and..." He trails off awkwardly, lowering his eyes to his glass, suddenly transfixed by the amber liquid inside. When she doesn't immediately respond, he sighs, downs the drink, and says, "Carry on, then. I won't keep you from your cooking. I'll try to check in again tomorrow night after my—"

"Tomorrow night?" West shoots him an incredulous glare. "Oh, I don't *think* so, Draegan."

He returns the look with a raised eyebrow. "I beg your pardon?"

"We're doing this now? Okay. I guess we're doing this now. Ever since the crash, the only topic you seem capable of discussing with me is whether I'm okay."

A muscle in his jaw ticks. "Because I'm concerned about your well-being. Is that a crime now?"

"You ask if I'm well," she barrels on. "You ask if I need drugs or bandages or pillows—pillows, Draegan! But you know what I *actually* need? The one thing missing? A night of normalcy. Well, as normal as things ever get here at Blackmoor. I just..." With a sigh, she crosses the kitchen to stand before him, and—surprising the hell out of me and Drae both—takes his hands. "I would *really* love it if we could all sit down and enjoy a meal together. One where no one asks if I'm okay, and no one argues about things that don't matter, and no one avoids each other because they feel awkward or guilty about things they absolutely shouldn't, because I certainly don't."

I have no idea whether she's referring to Drae's guilt over the crash and her battle with the mages, or something else entirely, but she's managed to bring an actual blush to his stern face.

"This isn't about... I'm just..." Draegan closes his eyes, gently shaking his head. Then, meeting her gaze again, "You're right, Miss Avery. I'm sorry. I've been... avoidant."

She squeezes his hands, her eyes imploring. "Come to dinner, Draegan. It won't be ready for a couple of hours yet, so you've still got plenty of time to go upstairs and make your important calls or... you know. Iron your wings. But we'd really love for you to join us."

At this, the man finally manages a small laugh, the wings rippling behind him. "Iron my wings. Yes, I suppose they could use a good pressing." He holds her gaze for another beat, then releases her hands and tucks an affectionate finger under her chin. "I'll be there. I promise."

When I hear Drae's bedroom door close upstairs, I smirk at West and say, "You planning on talking about it, or are we just going to keep pretending nothing's going on between you and Drae?"

"You already know what's going on." She hops up on the countertop again. "He's Broody McBrooderson, and I'm just trying to keep him from succumbing to an immortal life of eternal sulking."

"And his current round of brooding has nothing to do with any... *attraction* between the two of you?"

"What?" She huffs out an indignant breath, her eyes looking everywhere but at me. "No. No way. Draegan and me? That's just—"

I pop an olive into her mouth. "Denial."

West rolls her eyes. "Fine. Fine! Ugh. We did it. Happy now? Draegan and I did it the other night and now he's being weird and... What in the name of the Morrigan are you smiling about? I admitted it, okay? No need to rub it in."

"I'm not rubbing it in, witchling. I'm just glad the bastard finally admitted he has actual feelings for you, even if he's acting like a world-class dickhead about it now."

"He hasn't admitted *anything*. It was just... just a bit of fun, nothing more."

"A bit of fun that has your heart racing just mentioning it? And you're not even giving me any good details. Must've been some night."

She blows out a breath. "I mean... It was pretty intense. You know how he gets."

"Not in bed, I don't."

"Well, just picture him in every other situation you've ever witnessed, and extrapolate. It's not hard to imagine, Augs."

I grab a potholder and lift the lid on the bubbling sauce,

giving it another stir. "Let's see... Bossy and demanding, with a firm hand and epic control-freak tendencies that are quick to unravel... Oh! And let's not forget—completely closed-off emotionally with rare and fleeting glimpses of an actual heart, leaving you eager for more and questioning your own sanity as a result."

She gives me the finger guns. "Ding-ding-ding! Hashtag accurate! We have a winner, folks."

"West." I toss the potholder on the stove and take her face in my hands. "Drae's a damn fool, obviously. But he *does* have a heart. I know for a fact he cares about you."

"He told you that?"

"Didn't have to. I've known Draegan a long time. I can read him better than he can read himself. You're just... It's a lot for him to process. Doesn't help that his brain is just a hunk of solid stone now—doesn't turn back at sunset with the rest of his body."

A laugh escapes, her mood brightening considerably.

"And now, my witchling, you and I have an important decision to make."

"About Draegan?"

"Way more important than that. We need to pick the rest of the lasagna filling." I open the fridge, scanning the recently stocked shelves. "Let's see, we've got soy crumbles, vegan sausage—"

"Fake meat? For an Italian feast?" She gasps, her eyes wide with mock horror. "Augustine Lamont, the owners of this place should revoke your head chef status. A mix of finely chopped portobello mushrooms and red peppers is the *only* acceptable answer here."

I press a hand to my heart, gazing at her with open admiration. "Westlyn Avery, I think I just came."

"Not near the food, I hope. That's a serious health code violation."

"But not one of your food allergies. We've tested that out more than enough times to be sure."

A devious grin curves her lips. "I don't know, Augs. You can never be too certain. Allergies evolve all the time."

"You're right. We should probably test it again, just to be on the safe side."

She laughs again, and I capture it with a kiss, losing myself in the soft heat of her mouth, in the gentle slide of her tongue against mine. Her fingers thread into my hair, gently curling around my horns as my cock stirs between her thighs...

"Auggie," she pants, breaking for air, but I'm not ready to let her go just yet.

I claim her again, my kiss deeper, more devastating.

She pulls back, pawing at my chest. "Burning—"

"Me too, witchling. You're too fucking hot for your own good. You—"

"Not me, Top Chef! The stove!" She finally breaks out of my hold and hops off the counter, making a mad dash for the stove. "The potholder is literally on fire!"

~

Tragic potholder death aside, our Italian feast is a smashing success. The whole spread looks beautiful on the table, and West even lets me take a few photos of the presentation before ringing the proverbial dinner bell. Draegan shows up as promised, with Jude and Rook not far behind. The wine never stops flowing. And I can't recall a time when my boys loved one of my dishes so much they didn't leave so much as a single bite of leftovers.

Between sips of wine and nibbles on the last of the lasagna, Rook and West eagerly update everyone on the new intel they dug up on Zorakkov, along with the ever-deepening mysteries of the Codex and the still-elusive Spell of Unmaking. The fact that West has been able to tap into her magic on command for two nights running has us all raising a glass.

She and Rook seem especially cozy tonight, his wing drawn protectively around her shoulders, her body angled toward him, her eyes lighting up whenever he explains a particularly complex bit of demon lore.

I'm glad they're getting closer. She has a way with our resident genius—a sweetness that's drawn him out of a shell fifteen hundred years in the making.

Jude can't take his eyes off her, either, which doesn't surprise me. He was the first of us to cross her path, and he's been obsessed with her ever since.

Even Draegan's let down his guard a bit tonight, which feels like a rare chance to see the damn sunrise again.

It's hands down the best dinner we've ever had at Blackmoor. Not just because our sage-tomato sauce is restaurant-worthy, which, let's face it. *Obviously.*

But because all of us are gathered here, sitting at the same table, at the same time, laughing and drinking and truly enjoying each other's company.

This is family...

The thought comes unbidden, followed immediately by another one, even more powerful than the first—so intense it steals my breath and nearly brings me to my knees with the sudden force of wanting it so, so badly.

This is my *family.*

I take another moment to look at them. To appreciate this moment and how far we've come since the dark fae cursed us.

To appreciate what West has brought into our lives, however much of them we've got left.

But all too soon, the wine finally runs dry, and Draegan rises from the table in a way that makes it clear he's reached his limit. No explanation, no apologies. Just a simple thanks for the meal, and then he's leaving us again, his great talons clicking on the hardwood floors as he makes his way upstairs in a shroud of dark silence.

And the light that had been shining in West's eyes from the moment he first promised to join us tonight finally gutters out.

CHAPTER SEVENTEEN

JUDE

I don't care what's going on in that thick head of his.

I don't care how long I've known him or how loyal he's been to us.

I don't care how many calls he has to make or how many urgent matters he needs to attend to.

If Draegan Caldwell puts that sadness in our girl's eyes one more fucking time, I swear to the fucking *devil*...

"Come with me, darling." I rise from the table and hold out a hand, determined to bring her back to the light.

She blinks up at me for a moment. "Where?"

"The study."

"Why?"

I pull her to her feet. "To engage in a rousing game of Parcheesi, of course, followed by an intense debate about the merits of cryptocurrency in an unstable financial—"

"*Jude*. Be serious, for once."

"If you insist." With a sharp grin, I lower my mouth to her ear and whisper, "We're going to the study so I can lay you down in front of the fireplace, wrench your thighs apart, and fuck your tight little arse while Augustine eats your cunt for dessert. Rook, obviously, will bear witness. I do hope that's serious enough for you."

The breath rushes from her lungs, and I scoop her up off her feet before the poor girl faints.

"Would you like that, darling?" I ask.

"Yes," she whispers, some of the light returning to her eyes. "Much better than Parcheesi."

With the boys taking point, I carry our witch to the study. Augs is one step ahead of me, already spreading out the sofa blankets on the floor.

Rook, on the other hand, heads straight for the bar, wordlessly pouring himself a healthy dose of whatever booze he can grab first.

"Rook." I glance over my shoulder as I gently lay West on the blankets. "Am I right in assuming you're still playing silent observer to our nature show? Or are you downing some liquid courage over there in preparation for joining us?"

His clawed fingers tighten around his glass, but he doesn't move. Just watches us with heavy-lidded eyes, his heart rate kicking up a few notches.

Guess I've got my answer.

"Suit yourself, then. Best get comfortable, though. We're putting on one hell of a good show."

"Well! Look who's back." I've only just gotten my little scarecrow into position on her knees in front of me, her bare arse rubbing tantalizingly against my cock, Auggie flat on his back beneath her, when our resident bastard decides to grace us with his return. "Draegan. Is there something we can help you with?"

He takes in the scene—the three of us naked before the fire, my hands full of Westlyn's tits, Auggie's claws scraping against her thighs—and blinks rapidly, as if he can't quite figure out what's happening here. "I thought we might... have an apéritif together. But clearly..." He glances over at Rook, then back to me, clearing his throat. Jealousy flares in his eyes. "Sorry. I'll just be on my way, then."

"*You*," I say firmly, "will do no such thing."

If he's taken aback by my tone, he doesn't show it. With a deeply put-upon sigh, he says, "What do you *want*, Jude? Clearly you have better things to do than—"

"What I *want*, *Draegan*... What I truly, madly, *desperately* want... is to watch our beautiful girl suck your cock while I bury myself in her arse and Auggie puts his gourmet tongue to use licking every inch of her sweet—"

"Oh, is that all?" A calm, cool laugh hisses through

Drae's lips, but his eyes are dark with unspoken desire. "Sounds like a real family affair."

"Our witchling likes to share," Auggie says, running his hands up her inner thighs, his thumbs brushing her clit. "Don't you?"

Her body jolts at the contact, and I graze my palms over her nipples, enjoying the eruption of gooseflesh that follows.

"Goddess, yes," she whispers. Then, in a soft, angel-sweet voice, she says to Draegan, "Won't you join us tonight... Daddy?"

Draegan's steely resolve wavers. I can hear the erratic skip of his heart, the shortening of his breaths.

He takes a step closer. Then another.

Westlyn's face tilts back at his approach, like a flower drawn to the sun.

"And what of Rook?" he asks, peering down at her, his eyes dark and dangerous in the firelight. "Doesn't he get a spot in this lineup of tag-team debauchery?"

"Now, Draegan," I say. "You know our resident genius is a bit shy about girls who don't live in his computer. Don't force the issue. Besides, if there's one thing our girl loves almost as much as she loves sharing, it's being watched." I nip her earlobe. "And Rook *loves* watching."

Behind the bar, Rook has gone so still I'd swear he'd already turned to stone for the night if not for the heat in his eyes, the slight tremble of the liquid in his glass.

"I've seen you watching her, too, Draegan," I say, my

voice laced with quiet steel. "Seen the way you stare at this lush little mouth. So soft and warm and wet. So..." I trail my hand up her throat and push my fingers between her lips, in and out and in once more, her hot little tongue sliding over my skin. "...*Fuckable*."

Draegan's cock bulges. He doesn't bother trying to hide it.

"I know what you're thinking," I continue softly. "I can read it in your expression. In the greedy way you're looking at her, your mouth already watering for it. So go ahead, Draegan. Look me in the eyes and tell me you don't want these perfect lips wrapped around your cock tonight, sucking you until you spill down her throat while Augustine and I make her *beg* for release."

He glares at me for another beat, the rage inside him rising and crackling like the fire before us, then shifts his vicious gaze to Westlyn's mouth. I slide my fingers out, dragging a soft, seductive moan from her lips.

The rage in Draegan's eyes melts into pure lust, the last of his high-and-mighty resolve shattering. He grips her jaw, his clawed fingers trembling.

"Open your mouth," he commands, and she obeys him without question. With his free hand, he drops his loincloth and fists his cock, the tip already glistening with pre-cum.

Her tongue darts out, barely grazing his flesh.

Draegan hisses, his eyes rolling back. "You're... you're a dirty little girl, aren't you?"

"Only for my gargoyles, Daddy."

He curses under his breath, and his grip on her jaw tightens, his cock bobbing before her, brushing against her lips.

"Lick it for me," he whispers, and once again she obeys him, replacing his fist with her own at its base and swirling her tongue around the tip, then dragging it up and down his shaft.

"That's it," he breathes, falling deeper under her spell. "That's... just... right there, love. Just like that."

While Draegan takes a moment to get comfortable with his... *ahem*... new reality, I skim my hand down the front of Westlyn's body, greedily dipping between her thighs before Auggie takes his turn. Skin coated in her arousal, I shift my attention to her backside, gently working in one slick finger, then another, as Auggie unfurls his tongue and traces a slow circle around her clit.

Westlyn hums with pleasure, her body relaxing instantly for me, easily taking in another finger. I plumb deeper, stretching her, a silent warning of what's to come.

"Open wider for me," Draegan murmurs. "Show me how much more of Daddy's cock you can take."

Fuck me, I have no idea when this little daddy game started between them, but the way she's responding to his filthy commands has me so bloody turned on right now, I'm damn near seeing stars.

My dick is more than ready to come off the bench.

Certain she's relaxed enough to take it, I grip the base

and ease the tip into her arse, giving her a moment to adjust. I feel Auggie's tongue thrusting inside her now, his grip on her thighs tightening and spreading her wider as he enjoys his fine dessert.

"That's it," Draegan whispers. "Deeper. Relax your throat and... yes. Now suck it for me. Harder. Just like... *fuck*. *Just* like that. Bloody hell, little mortal. You're so... so fucking good. Such a good fucking girl."

At his stammering words of praise, the little scarecrow moans again, and I slide in deeper, her body tightening around my cock, taking me all the way in.

Bloody *hell*, she feels so fucking good. So soft and warm and perfect and... fuck, I can't get enough of her.

None of us can.

Between her thighs, Auggie continues feasting on her like a starved animal, every kiss and lick and hot, desperate breath making her come a little more undone. Draegan's got his hands in her hair, his grip tight as he fucks her wet mouth and I plunder her tight little arse, fucking her deeper, harder, the fire raging on.

And Westlyn... What a fucking sight to behold.

"You're so lovely, darling," I whisper. "Taking all three of us, putting on a show for Rook. I wish you could see how beautiful you are right now. And this hair..." I gather her dark waves in my hands and bury my face in it, taking a deep breath of her sweet apple scent. "Devils *balls*, I love your fucking hair."

A soft moan is all I get in response, her mouth so perfectly filled with Draegan's cock she can't speak. She arches her back and grinds down on Auggie's face as he devours her with his mouth, and I match every roll and dip of her hips with another deep thrust, and all the while, our spymaster watches from across the room. Rapt. Captivated.

Hard.

I bury my face in her hair again, then kiss her neck, her shoulder, grazing her skin with my fangs before sucking it between my lips, the salt of her sweat making me harder... so *fucking* hard for her I worry she won't be able to take much more of me...

Snaking an arm around her waist, I say softly, "Tap my arm twice if you want out."

She wraps her fingers around it, but doesn't tap. Just rolls her hips back to meet my next thrust, eager as ever for more, more, more.

I wrap my other hand around her throat, her rapid-fire pulse fluttering against my palm, throat bobbing as she tries to swallow the rest of Draegan's massive cock.

"Relax," Draegan says again. "Breathe through your nose and... Fuck, that's it. You can take it. I know you can take all of it for Daddy... That's... yes... *fuck*, I'm so... so close..."

I feel his every thrust, his commands growing more urgent, but she's the one in charge now, his control unraveling like she's finally found the one loose thread in his composure and given it a good yank.

Her throat constricts as she fights not to gag, hot

tears slipping down her cheeks and splashing onto my hand, but she's not tapping out. Far from it. She's riding Auggie's face harder and faster, chasing the release he's so close to giving her, her tits bouncing as I slam into her arse, Draegan fisting her hair and owning her lush mouth with a final, impossibly deep thrust, and then...

She tightens around my cock and unleashes a wild moan of pleasure, coming on Auggie's tongue just as Draegan reaches the same blissful edge.

"*Westlyn*," he grinds out, and I feel her throat working harder beneath my grip. "Right there... just like that... oh, *fuck*..."

His body goes still, a tremor rippling through him as he comes hot and hard, his eyes closed tight, the muscles in his arms tense and bulging, Westlyn swallowing down every drop.

After a few more moments, he finally pulls out of her mouth and sucks in a shuddering breath, swaying on his feet.

Her back pressed against my chest, my cock buried deep inside her, Westlyn rises up higher on her knees, and Auggie slides out from beneath her, his mouth and chin shining with the evidence of her intense pleasure.

I slow my thrusts, dragging my cock almost all the way out, then slowly gliding back in, holding off on my own release, my balls fucking *begging* for it, but no. Not yet.

I'm not ready for this to end.

Draegan peers down at Westlyn's face, his expression utterly dazed.

"Kiss me," she whispers, but the bastard merely shakes his head.

"Daddy's not finished with that mouth yet, little mortal." Gripping her jaw again, he glances at Auggie and says darkly, "I want to see what you look like with another man's cock fucking your throat."

Westlyn gasps, and I tighten my arm around her waist, reminding her she can call it off whenever she wants.

But bloody hell, she's into this. Draegan's into this. *I'm* into this. We're all fucking into this, and now Auggie's on his feet too, standing next to Drae and fisting his rock-hard cock.

"Give it to her, Augustine," Draegan says.

Auggie looks to West, who nods and reaches for him. The moment his cock touches her swollen lips, Drae grips a handful of her hair and says, "Open your mouth and *suck*."

And fuck, she does exactly what he says, taking Auggie in deep, massaging his balls as she works his cock with her lips and tongue, her throat, everything she's got.

Her body heats up in my arms again, the scent of her desire spiking hard. I bring my tail around between the front of her thighs, gently rubbing her clit as I fuck her, my control slipping, my cock driving relentlessly into her arse, my tail sliding over her hot, wet flesh as Draegan commands her to take it deeper, to suck, to swallow...

Auggie can't hold out another minute. With a roar, he

comes down her throat, his cock slipping out of her mouth and spilling more hot cum down her chest. The sight of it makes Draegan rock fucking hard again. West doesn't miss a beat; Auggie's barely finished painting her when she grabs Draegan's cock, and he arches into her hand, fucking her tight little fist with hard, angry thrusts, as if he can't stand the fact that he cares for her. That he wants this as badly as the rest of us, and he's determined to take out every last one of his frustrations on her.

My balls tingle, and I know I've got maybe five more seconds...

"Let me taste you again, Daddy," she whispers, and before Draegan can even process it, she's got her lips wrapped around his cock again, sucking him in deep, and without so much as a shudder in warning, he fucking unloads.

She tightens around my cock, and I increase the friction on her clit with my tail, pushing her right back over the cliff.

She comes with a deep, rumbling groan that vibrates through her entire body, setting off a chain reaction that explodes inside me, lighting my nerves on fire. I grip her hips and fuck and fuck and *fuck* until I finally detonate, coming inside her arse with a force that leaves me dizzy and spent and halfway to death's fucking door.

Draegan stumbles backward onto the sofa, and the rest of us collapse in a pile on the blankets, staring up at the ceiling and waiting for our souls to return to our bodies.

Rook doesn't move. Doesn't even fucking breathe.

It's an eternity before I can see straight again, and when the haze finally clears, I lift my head and find Draegan staring at us, his expression unreadable. He catches my gaze and holds it.

The intensity burning in his eyes is shocking.

"Draegan," West murmurs beside me. "I'm still waiting for my kiss."

Draegan doesn't reply. Spares her a momentary glance, cold and indifferent. Then he's looking at me again.

Something passes between us. Some shared understanding. An admission on his part. An acceptance on mine.

He feels it, too. This inexplicable connection that goes beyond infatuation or obsession. Beyond a good time. Beyond one more roll in the sheets before the curse finally destroys us.

It isn't even just love. Not any more.

The four of us are connected to her on a *soul* level. Eternally bound.

But he'll never be able to say it out loud. Never be able to welcome it into his heart.

This, I know.

He nods at me once. I return it.

Wordlessly, he gets to his feet, grabs his loincloth, and stalks out of the room.

Westlyn sits up next to me and sighs, a shiver rolling through her body.

"Cold, darling?" I pull up one of the blankets and drape it over her shoulders, rubbing some warmth into her back. She leans into my touch, and I take another minute to breathe her in, the taste of her skin still fresh on my lips.

It's barely another minute before she pulls away, pressing a soft kiss to my cheek and getting to her feet.

"Are you all right, scarecrow?" I ask. "You seem a bit off. Did we... Was it too much this time?"

A soft smile. A warm blush. "No."

"Look, don't worry about Drae. He's just not good with... feelings. Of any sort. You've likely short-circuited his delicate wiring with that naughty little tongue of yours."

She forces another smile, but I know she doesn't mean it. "I'm okay. I just need a hot shower. I'll be back down in a bit."

"Trying to wash me away already?"

"I'm sure you'll make a mess of me again later."

"It's a date, then." I wink and smack her on the fine arse, and then she's off.

"Drae's a dick," Auggie says, once she's out of earshot.

"Huge one," I concur. "Biggest I've ever seen."

"Pretty sure I'm gonna beat his ass tomorrow night, if you want in. Just trying to finalize my approach."

I laugh. I'm about to take him up on the offer when a shrill beep sounds off near the bar.

Rook.

He finally snaps out of his trance, frantically snatching his phone off the bar.

Glancing at the screen, he gasps.

"What the bloody hell is that?" I ask.

"The alarm on the code-breaker I built. I just cracked the encryption on the SSD card." He looks up at us with a wide grin. "We're in."

CHAPTER EIGHTEEN

DRAEGAN

I don't know why I'm lingering outside her door.

Clearly, she'd rather be left alone.

And for my part, Westlyn Avery is the last person I want to see right now, anyway.

But she's also the *only* person I want to see right now.

The paradox is splitting my skull.

Fuck. My head's a mess, my heart's tangled up in thorns, and I've got absolutely *no* business disturbing her. No right to ask after her wellbeing when it's generally my fault she's unwell in the first place.

Guilt chews through my gut. The pained look in her eyes tonight when I refused to kiss her for a second time... Bloody hell, the memory of it is a curse that will haunt me more deeply than the one that turned us all to stone.

Because unlike that ancient spell, *this* agony is something I could've prevented.

Apologize to her, you daft bastard. Apologize, and then you can both get back to politely avoiding each other like you did in the good ol' days...

I knock softly, and she invites me in, her voice sweet. For that brief moment my heart lifts—perhaps I didn't wound her as deeply as I'd feared—but the instant she sees me entering, her face falls, taking my hope down along with it.

Clearly, she thought I was one of the others. Anyone but the gargoyle who keeps her at arm's length, reeling her in when it suits him, only to toss her back out to sea the moment things get the slightest bit uncomfortable for him.

That's what she sees when she looks at me now, and I don't blame her.

"Draegan," she whispers, and I try to pretend it's not disappointment lacing her voice. "Is everything okay?"

I watch her for a moment, sitting on her bed in a pair of lavender shorts and a cropped hooded sweatshirt, her cheeks pink, her just-washed hair dampening the fabric around her shoulders. She's lit a few candles on her bedside table, the warm light flickering in golden hues on her face.

Devil's balls, how did it come to this? To this fierce, fiery woman crashing into our lives and upending everything I thought I knew, thought I *wanted* out of whatever time we had left, only to leave me feeling as helpless as I did the night the dark fae destroyed us?

I can't deny the connection I felt to her—right from the very start, just like the others. I've always known there was more to it than a simple appreciation for a beautiful woman. More to it than lust or curiosity or even a gargoyle's protective instincts.

But *this*? No. She has utterly invaded me. I'm *drowning* in her, and I don't remember how to breathe.

"No," I finally reply. "It isn't. There's... something I need to tell you. Many things, actually. Only... I'm not quite sure I know where to start."

One of her ravens—Lucinda, I think—hops up on the bed beside her, nuzzling her bare thigh.

Westlyn twists the wet locks of her hair into a braid and sighs.

"You could start by telling me why you left like that," she says softly. There's no accusation in her tone, no bitterness. Just a simple request for an answer that's far more complex than she could ever imagine.

"I didn't mean to upset you," I reply.

"Well first of all, mission *not* accomplished, because you *did* upset me. And second of all..." She sighs, the weight of it landing on my shoulders. "That's not an answer, Draegan. Just another attempt at evasion."

"I know, little mortal. I know."

Hell. Why is this so damned hard? Why can't I take what she's so earnestly offering me? I've never felt so at peace, so whole as I do when she's in my arms. And yet I resist it with every bit of strength I possess.

My heart is going to rip in two.

"Draegan, why are things still so... so tense between us?"

She finally looks up to meet my gaze. Tears glitter on her cheeks, each one burning a fresh hole in my heart, knowing I'm the reason for them. "I'm trying to understand you, but every time I feel us getting closer, something happens and you just... You clam right up again. Or you disappear completely, leaving me to wonder what the hell I said or did to—"

"It's nothing you said or did, Miss Avery. Never. It's... it's complicated and I..." I trail off, hating how trite the words sound. *It's complicated?* She deserves better than this. Better than *me*.

"I care for you," she says. "More than I probably should, given all the red flags. And I *like* being with you like... like how we were tonight. And that night in your office. But if you're not cool with the physical stuff, that's okay. I mean it, Draegan. We can just be friends if that's what you want. I'm not expecting anything from you aside from honesty and respect."

"You've got both—I assure you. Along with my vow to keep you safe—*that* is unshakeable."

She closes her eyes as another sigh escapes. "Because you're a gargoyle. Yes, I know how it works."

I cross the room and sit on the edge of the bed beside her. Lucinda squawks at me, then finally toddles off in search of something more interesting.

Taking her hand, I say softly, "Because I care about you, too. More than I probably should." I smile, but I can't hold on to it for more than a moment.

"And the other stuff? The sex? Is that... not something you're into?" A soft blush darkens her cheeks, but she doesn't falter, her gaze holding mine in the flickering candlelight.

Those eyes have the power to incinerate me and send me straight to hell, but I can't look away.

I never could—not really.

Not that night in my office. Not tonight, watching the others touch her, taste her. Seeing the pure, undiluted pleasure rise on her face in shades that match my memories of the brilliant dawn sky.

"I'm... not quite sure I've ever been into anything more, Miss Avery," I reply honestly. I make another attempt at a smile, but once again it falters in the wake of her melancholy.

"Then why did you leave like that?" she asks. "One minute we were all together and everything was perfect and... I don't understand. It's like you resent everyone—that's the feeling I get. And I'm honestly trying to figure out why."

I reach up to erase one of her tears, my palm lingering on her smooth cheek. "I *am* resentful."

"But... why?"

It's a long time before I'm able to respond, and when the honest words finally come to me, every one of them cuts like broken glass as it passes through my lips. "Because they're... they're happy now. You... you make them happy."

I know it doesn't make sense to her—hell, it barely makes sense to me. But it's the truth.

Just not all of it.

I lower my hand and take a deep breath, knowing I owe her more.

"Miss Avery. Westlyn... You have brought more joy to our lives in a month than we've experienced in centuries. Augustine is cooking again, and I found him in the orchard the other night, photographing the apple trees and a family of owls—*beautiful* things, not just the gargoyles we mourn or the men we seek to break. Jude, for all his violent tendencies, is damn near serene, by his standards. Rook... Well, I don't recall seeing that gargoyle much at all outside the library or his gaming lair in the past, and I swear I haven't seen him truly smile in centuries. Yet now he walks around with a perpetual grin and a twinkle in his eye. And that—all of it—is thanks to your presence among us."

"And what about you?" She takes my hand again, the fire back in her eyes. "Has my presence done anything besides make your life more difficult? Because that's how it feels lately."

I lower my eyes, shame heating my face.

"Draegan," she whispers, her breath feathering across my lips. "What are you so afraid of?"

"I'm afraid of... I..." A single tear slips down my cheek, and I swallow hard, all those sharp glass edges slicing me anew. Forcing myself to look into her eyes again, I cup her cheek and say softly, "When I look at you, when I hear your laughter, when I touch you, I feel myself... falling and I... It is a thing I simply *cannot* allow."

Her mouth parts, emotion gathering in her eyes like a storm.

"Westlyn, you... you need to know the truth about me. About us. The past and the curse. What it truly means."

Her eyes widen, and I press on, forcing myself to keep going.

"You know it's not just my story, but it *is* my duty to tell you."

"Why?" she asks.

"Because what happened to us is my fault." I take her hand, and in the center, I drop the heart-shape stone I've kept by my bedside every night since it was given to me as a man. "This was given to me by someone very special to me. It's... it's the only thing I've managed to keep from... before."

She nods, and I realize she's likely seen it before, every night she's spent recovering in my bed. I've never hidden it.

"A.C." She traces over the carved letters with a light touch. "Are they initials?"

I nod, bracing myself for what comes next. "Anastasia Caldwell. She was... She *is*... Anastasia is my daughter, Westlyn."

Anastasia. Daughter. The words are foreign on my tongue, the taste of them like blood and ash coating the back of my throat. I haven't said either aloud in centuries. There was no need; my men knew her as a human girl. Played with her.

Chased her around the barley fields until happy exhaustion finally overtook her.

They grieved her as I did, as we grieved all the ones we lost.

And in the time since our banishment began, no one has ever earned my trust enough to hear her name or what she was to me—until now.

Tears fall from Westlyn's eyes in earnest. She doesn't speak, and I spare her the agony of trying to find words for a horror that can never be eased with them anyway, instead filling the silence that follows with the story of how her gargoyles came to be.

CHAPTER NINETEEN

DRAEGAN

"The gargoyles and I—Rook, Jude, Augustine, and all the stone creatures of this city we've worked so hard to protect—we were men of Britain once. Humans. Friends and neighbors in the village of Blackmoor and the surrounding towns, fifteen hundred years ago."

Westlyn gasps.

"I know we don't look quite that ancient," I say. "But sometimes, Westlyn... Sometimes I feel the weight of those years with every breath. Like my bones understand they were meant to turn to dust long ago and still resent me for making them carry me around all these centuries."

She curls her fingers protectively around the stone, her eyes never leaving mine.

"In those days," I continue, "most mortals still believed in magic. We knew the fae were real even if we couldn't see them—we'd all grown up with stories of the so-called 'good neighbors.' And for the most part, we knew better than to provoke them into showing themselves. It was best, we all agreed, to silently acknowledge them, respect them from a distance, and allow our kinds to peacefully co-exist. But over time, humans became more brazen, intentionally taunting the fae, luring them into traps and forcing them to reveal their secrets. Their magic."

Anger flashes in her eyes. "Goddess, this is a recurring theme in all Rook's library books, too. Wherever something rare and magical is found, humans aren't far behind, lining up to trample it."

"Never underestimate mankind's unique ability to destroy the things they can't control or understand." One of the candles sputters out, and I reach over to re-light it with one of the others. "Eventually, the fae grew tired of the torment, and called upon their dark kin for aid—dark fae of the Wintermoon court and its vile king, Verrick."

Goosebumps pebble Westlyn's bare legs, a chill vibrating through her body, head to toe. All the color bleaches from her face.

Wintermoon has that effect.

"It was a desperate measure, even for them," I say.

"How do you mean?"

"The dark fae aren't like the others. *All* fae are tricksters, most of them cruel ones at that. But the dark fae of Wintermoon are downright *murderous*. They have no love for mankind—never have. When they heard of the atrocities humans were committing against their kin, Verrick mounted a swift, coordinated attack."

"On your lands?"

I nod. "I was a blacksmith and owned an armory—the Blackmoor man with the most military experience, as limited as it was. I led the human resistance, with Jude, Augustine, and Rook—my most trusted friends—serving as my commanders. Together with the surrounding towns and villages, we cobbled together an army of human soldiers willing to fight."

"A war. An actual war between the dark fae and humans —*your* humans. Draegan, that's... I can't believe it."

"The story of the war itself is a long and bloody tale, but after four brutal years, we finally achieved victory. The Wintermoon king very well could have beaten us, but he hadn't expected to encounter such a steadfast resistance at all, and eventually he grew tired of sacrificing fae soldiers for what amounted to little more than a game to him. He called back his armies and ceded control of our lands. In exchange, we would allow the fae to come and go as they had for millennia, without interference or harassment from us. We thought that was the end of it and agreed to the terms, but dark fae being who they are..."

"There was a loophole," she whispers. "A trick."

"We could keep the land, Verrick informed us. But unless we accepted the rest of his terms, he would burn the crops and homes and slaughter the animals, effectively starving us out."

"What did he want?"

I close my eyes, a familiar black cloud churning inside me. "The men who led the humans to victory against his armies. Jude, Rook, Augustine, and me... We offered ourselves up as sacrifices, thinking that would be enough. The commanders. The leader. But he wanted more. More. *More*, until all the men who took up arms against the fae for miles around were finally in his custody. Not as prisoners to be executed, no. That would've been too kind a punishment. He had a different sentence in mind for us."

Silence falls between us again, the fluttering candles casting dark shadows on the walls. She knows now where this part of the story is heading. Sees its crushing, inevitable end on the near horizon.

"As leaders of the resistance who so steadfastly guarded human lands," I continue, "King Verrick thought it fitting that we become the immortal guardians of Wintermoon, guarding its most powerful portals to the human realm for all eternity."

"Gargoyles," she breathes.

"With a combination of demonic magic and their own, they crafted a spell that created the very first ones. Immortal monsters that would appear to others as fae, but were actually ferocious winged beasts who could turn to stone at will, *forced* into stone by daybreak. They positioned gargoyles throughout the world, assigned to all the places Wintermoon armies wanted to invade."

"But I thought he ceded human lands to the humans?"

"No. Only the lands of Britain—another loophole. The rest of the human world was fair game, as far as he was concerned. And now, thanks to his personal force of immortal guardians, he could ensure the dark fae could come and go as they pleased. Any humans who disturbed them—who so much as looked too closely at them—were simply..." *Murdered.* I can't bring myself to say the word out loud. Can't bring myself to recount the number of humans I killed at Verrick's behest.

"But, over time," I continue, "as the human population grew and began encroaching on the natural world, it became harder for the fae to travel to this realm. They require nature—it's a deeply inherent part of their life force, their magic. The portals began failing. In his rage, Verrick blamed his guardians for the failures. For any portal he could no longer safely access, he turned its gargoyle keeper into permanent stone."

"Goddess," she whispers. "Do they die?"

"Death would be better. It merely traps the once-human soul for eternity."

"What happens if the stone gargoyle itself is destroyed? Does that free its soul?"

I shake my head, the reminder of that cruel fate twisting me up inside. "Unless we can break the curse, a stone gargoyle destroyed means his soul is simply cursed to wander the realms, never finding peace, never able to speak with or touch another. Just... existing."

She reaches for my hand again, lacing our fingers together and holding tight.

"Our numbers dwindled overseas," I say. "With more and more portals failing as cities continued to expand all over Europe and Asia, Verrick grew restless. Concerned about his options in a realm that seemed intent on building, he relocated the remaining gargoyles to the Americas. But of course, the same thing was happening here. Colonization, expansion, wholesale slaughter of life, destruction of natural resources. Eventually, he decided to cut his losses and concentrate on a single geographic region, placing the four so-called war heroes in charge."

"New York," she says.

"Yes. Though it wasn't the New York you know now. The region was vast and beautiful, with rivers and mountains, forests... Verrick truly thought he'd found his next paradise. The four of us were tasked with guarding the guardians, so to speak. Well, you know what New York eventually became. All that concrete and steel and glass... It's nearly impossible for pureblooded dark fae to travel here now, let alone exist here for any length of time. So Verrick once again began turning his guardians to stone until eventually there were none left but us. We kept waiting for that fateful night when he'd turn his ire on the men who led armies against him, but it never came. We finally realized he'd intended it that way. *This* was our eternal punishment. Existing in a world where everyone we knew, everyone who fought for us and bled by our side on the battlefields of home, was nothing but a stone statue, magically bound to a portal that would exist for eternity, whether or not it would ever be accessed."

"But... how many portals are there?"

"I don't know exactly—many have been abandoned. But every gargoyle in this city guards a fae portal."

"How can they still guard the portals if they're cursed as permanent stone?"

"It's all part of the dark fae magic. Our souls serve as... well, the best way to think of it is like a power source. So the stone gargoyles... They're essentially keeping the lights on for the day Verrick decides to make his move."

"I thought he couldn't exist here long-term?"

"Not now, he can't. But one day—perhaps when humans are extinct and the land reclaims itself from the concrete—Verrick will get his opportunity. Fae are immortal, love. Tens of thousands of years is naught but a blink."

She's quiet again, processing everything I've told her.

Then, "You guys were from the same village," she says. "Why do you have such different accents?"

"That is partly choice, and partly where we've spent time and with whom. Our original accents are very different from the way most British people speak today anyway—using them wouldn't help us keep a low profile. Over time, our speech just... evolved, I guess. As all spoken language does."

And even if it hadn't, none of us would dare speak in the melodic cadence of home now. It's too painful.

"And Blackmoor—the company, not the village... That's why your firm buys up all the historic buildings?" she asks. "So you can... take care of your gargoyle friends?"

"Yes. As best we can, at least until we can find a way to break the curse and set our men free. Their souls, anyway."

"The... the men. You said they only took the men." Her eyes widen, and she looks up at me again with a gasp. "That's why there are no female gargoyles in the city. Auggie's photos... they're all male. You... you had to leave them behind. Your daughter and... your..."

"Moira," I say, my voice breaking. "My... My wife."

The raw horror that floods her eyes is enough to break me. "Verrick took you from them. He took you from your—"

"No." I press her palms together over the heart-shaped stone, my hands surrounding hers, and I close my eyes, not wanting to see what will certainly fill her gaze next. "The women of our villages were slaughtered, as were the..." My throat aches, but I force myself to carry on, to find the courage to say all these words out loud, even if all I can manage is a strangled whisper. "The children. They killed the children as well, along with the few elderly residents in our village. My... family. All of Rook's nieces and nephews. Jude's younger brothers. Augustine's elderly mother and aunt. They were not... kind or quick. The fields of our homeland ran red with the blood of our people until only the grown men and teenaged boys were left. The fighters."

The night goes still around us again, the sound of her

every ragged heartbeat nearly drowning out my own, and finally she slides her hands out from my hold and draws me into her embrace, her arms tight around me, and for that brief moment, I let all of my carefully built walls crumble.

I cling to her, burying my face against her neck, breathing in the scent of her skin as I whisper my deepest, darkest confession. "My wife and daughter were murdered, Westlyn. Anastasia... she was seven years old and so full of life... I swear to you, looking at her felt like looking at the sun. And now... It's been so long, I... I *know* I loved my family. But what has stayed with me all these centuries, what is more deeply imbedded in my heart than all the love and cherished memories I have of them... is the guilt. I should've been able to save them, to protect them. If I'd been stronger, if I'd been a better father and husband, if I'd—"

"Draegan," she whispers, her throat bobbing against my cheek. "You *did* protect them. You risked your life on the battlefield, and in the end, you sacrificed yourself to Verrick so that your family—your people—would have a shot at a better life. If that's not being a good father and husband, I don't know what is."

"They died, Westlyn. At the hands of a vicious king who took pleasure in their pain. In *my* pain."

"And if you hadn't fought against him, the invading dark fae would've done unspeakable things as well. You can't go back, Draegan. You can't rewrite history with your guilt."

I try to pull away, but she only tightens her hold, her

warm breath stirring my hair, her heartbeat settling into a steady thrum against my ear. And once again, I stop resisting and allow myself this momentary comfort, this simple joy of true human connection and compassion and friendship.

And there, bathed in rose-gold candlelight and wrapped in the arms of a woman who refuses to back down from a fight, I close my eyes and weep for all the ghosts in my heart.

CHAPTER TWENTY

ROOK

I hate that it's come to this.

All the mystery, all the secrecy, all the damn hope.

It took days, but I finally cracked the password. Finally unlocked one of our biggest clues to the mysteries of West's past—a past that could very well determine her future. After getting the alert on my phone and confirming it wasn't a false alarm, I've spent the last hour in the library, transferring all the files from the SSD card onto my tablet so she could see them for herself.

Now, all I want to do is pretend I never saw them. Pretend the card just couldn't be cracked. Pitch it into the flames and burn it to hell.

But I made a promise. We all did.

No secrets.

No matter how terrible. No matter how dangerous.

She deserves to know.

Loaded with the new files, my tablet feels like it weighs a hundred pounds, the heaviness of its dark revelations bearing down on me, crushing my lungs. I trudge back across the lawn toward the manor, toward the soft firelight glow of the study, where I know Jude and Auggie are awaiting my report.

"Well?" Jude gets to his feet the moment I step inside. Auggie was already pacing. "What did you find?"

I take a deep, steadying breath. Sex and desire linger in the air, the memories of what transpired tonight making me ache. Making me wish, once again, I could unknow all that I've learned.

"Letters," I finally manage. "Diaries. A mix of both."

"Whose diaries?" Auggie asks.

"Madison Strauss. West's mother—it seems she wrote them for her while West was in the womb. They're... they're about West's true lineage. About the danger she..." I trail off, my throat closing around the word.

Danger.

This whole time, I thought the threats she faced were because of who the shadow magic society *thought* she was. An augmenter. A witch with no power of her own who could only be used to further the goals of the corrupt arch-mage and his demon pets.

But the danger she faces is so much worse than that. Worse than her stepmother. Worse than the Forsythes and the mage bullies of her past.

Worse, I'm afraid, than even Zorakkov.

"You've read them?" Jude asks.

"Not all of them. Just the first couple—I didn't understand what they were at first. What they meant. Once I realized they were from her mother, I skimmed a few more, just to see if the files contained anything else, maybe something encoded within the letters themselves." I shake my head, setting my tablet on the sofa and heading for the bar. "I thought it would be best to let her read the rest on her own. Whatever she wants to share, that's her call."

"But that's... good news, isn't it?" Auggie asks, his face lined with concern and confusion. "Maybe now she can get to know her mom. Maybe even discover more about her bloodline and her magic."

I don't respond. Can't find the words just yet.

I reach for the whiskey. Pour a stiff glass and bring it to my lips, drawing in a deep drink.

"Rook." Jude's at my side, his hand curling around the top edge of my wing, eyes scrutinizing my face. "What aren't you telling us?"

I close my eyes and take another drink. Then, "Augustine, you've been sensing some kind of dark entity ever since we brought her here. Yes?"

"It comes and goes," he replies. "But yeah. I sensed it that night at the Ryker plant, too. And the night she was attacked in the woods. But I don't see what you're getting at here, Rook. Are you saying this entity is real? That it's... what? Attached itself to her, somehow?"

"Not attached." I set down my glass and meet his worried

gaze. "The dark entity... It *is* her, Auggie. A part of her she may not even recognize—a part that's lain dormant for most of her life, most likely muted by a binding rune someone gave her for that exact purpose." I pace as the realizations barrel through my mind, one right after the other. Her extreme reaction to the Midnight's Lullaby flowers in her wedding bouquet. The runes glowing on her skin. The reaction to a Codex containing dark fae magic. The real reason the demon wants her so badly.

"What the fuck are you on about?" Jude asks, and I realize I'm thinking all of this out loud, rambling a mile a minute.

"Think about it," I say. "West was led to believe she's a pureblood witch from a powerful family. Her mother was said to be one of the most powerful witches in an age, and her father was no slouch on that front either. Yet somehow, she's born with *zero* magic? Do you have any idea how rare that is?"

"Impossible," Auggie says. "That's how rare."

"But you already figured that bit out," Jude says. "Last night with the Codex, no? Westlyn was able to tap into her magic. She knows she's not an augmenter. She *does* have magic—just hasn't figured out how it all works yet."

"Yes, she has magic," I say. "But I don't think it's witch magic. At least, not all of it."

"What the fuck else would it be?" Jude scoffs. "Pixie dust? A bit of hocus pocus and—"

"Fae magic," I say. "Dark fae magic."

Jude's wings shiver. "That's... a bit of a jump. I mean, we know she's got a touch of dark fae blood back in the family tree, but... No. I'm not buying it. She's a witch, through and through. Half from mum, half from dad. Anything else in the genetic mix is inconsequential."

"All indications are she's the natural daughter of Madison Strauss," Auggie says, "who was a known and prominent witch. It's hard to fake an actual birth. And even though we know the shadow magic society had something to do with that birth—and it's connected to Hunter's treatments—what would be the point of them forging birth records and lying about her birthmother? Now, there's always a chance Brian Avery isn't her biological father, but we can't know that without a paternity test, right? And he's off the grid, so we—"

"We *can* know that." I sigh, the knot of dread tightening in my gut. "It was in the first letter, guys. Brian Avery *isn't* West's biological father. And she's more than a *touch* of dark fae, Jude. She's half."

"But... What?" He scratches behind his horns. "No. That would mean—"

"*Half*," I say again. "Fifty percent. The product of a witch mother and a full-blooded, dark-fae father. *That's* what it means."

"Fuck," he says.

"Fuck," Auggie echoes.

"Fuck is exactly right. And that?" I drop onto the couch,

a bitter laugh clawing its way up my throat. "That's the *good* news, I'm afraid."

"We've just learned our girl is half dark fae," Jude says, taking the seat next to me, "the evil part of her kept at bay by naught but a binding rune that may or may not be permanent, and if she's like most dark fae that part of her is probably programmed to kill us, and all of this likely means the damn mages and demons want her for some purpose we can't even *begin* to fathom, and *that's* the good news? What the bloody hell's the bad?"

"A thing for which there are not enough *fucks* in the world." I remove my glasses and close my eyes, tipping my head back against the sofa and wishing I could empty the whole thing out. "You're going to need to pour another round for this one, boys. Maybe even two."

CHAPTER TWENTY-ONE

DRAEGAN

By the time I feel like I can breathe again, the candles have burned down to stubs and the moon has risen high in the autumn sky.

When I find the courage to draw back and meet Westlyn's gaze, there's no mistaking what I see in her eyes.

Love.

Warmth rises inside, my heart expanding. But then, just like a balloon snagged on a rusty nail, it deflates.

You can't have this, Caldwell. It was never yours to want.

My walls go back up, brick by brick, and I turn away from her, desperately trying to gather the last of my thoughts.

Soft fingertips brush the edge of my wing, and I shudder.

"Westlyn." I take her hand in mine and turn back to look at her again. She's still holding my daughter's stone, and now it's warm from her touch, and her eyes are so full of hope—that dangerous, brittle thing I'm going to have to rip out from under her...

"Why are you looking at me like that?" she whispers.

"Like what?"

Another tear spills down her cheek. "Like you're about to break my heart."

Damn it. Why must I spell it out for her? Why can't she simply understand?

"You've brought so much happiness to this home," I say. "I've told you as much."

"And you resent it."

"Yes. Because for the first time since the fae cursed us with this *wretched* existence, you've made them—made *us*—want things we simply cannot have."

"No. You only *think* you can't have it because you're still punishing yourself for the sins of a dark fae murderer."

"That's not..." I take a deep breath and try again. "On the day Verrick slaughtered my family, my heart turned to stone—literally and figuratively. I thought I'd made peace with that—not with their deaths, never. But with my existence as an immortal gargoyle. My burden and what it meant to carry it in a city filled with men even more corrupt than the Wintermoon fae. Yet somehow, after fifteen hundred years of protecting the gargoyles in our care, fifteen hundred years of searching for a way to break our curse and set them free, one month with you has shattered *all* of that. The others have forgotten what it means to be cursed in this way. Forgotten that we are not allowed to live as mortals anymore. To *love* as mortals."

"You might not be willing to go there, but as for Rook and Auggie and Jude? It's not your call, Draegan. Who's to say they can't have this?"

"Our curse... it was never meant to be eternal. Verrick didn't intend for his guardians to live this long, even as immortals. He underestimated how long humanity would cling to its realm—that's the only reason the four of us still linger. The curse, eventually, will run its course, and we will turn to stone just like all the others."

"I don't know why we're even talking about this. We're going to *break* the curse, Draegan. We've already opened the Codex, and now we're transcribing it. We're so close to finding that Unmaking spell—I know it."

"Westlyn." I run my thumb along her palm, my touch as soft as my voice. "What do you suppose happens when we break the curse?"

"You're free. That's what we're working toward, right? That's our end game. Freedom."

"Freedom. Yes. And what do you think that means for your gargoyles?"

"I guess I just... I don't know. I figured once we broke the curse, you'd turn back into mortal men. The men you were *before* the curse. Which would mean you'd die *eventually*, but you could live out the rest of your days in *this* timeline, as humans. With... with me."

"There won't be any more days to live out. We won't

survive this curse. Even if you break it tomorrow, we won't survive it."

"You don't know that."

"I do." I cradle her cheeks, her lovely face blurring through the fresh tears glazing my eyes. "Freedom from this curse doesn't mean we get to live as the men we once were, love. Those men died centuries ago. All that remains of them is what you see before you now."

I unfurl my wings. My fangs descend, no doubt glinting in the candlelight.

"Gargoyles," she whispers, and I nod.

"End that, and what's left but—"

"Death." Tears spill down her cheeks, warm and wet on my thumbs. "You said death would be better. That's what you meant. That's what you *want*. Death."

"It's not what I want, little mortal. It's merely the better of two terrible outcomes."

"Then why are you trying to protect me?" She pulls out of my embrace and rises from the bed, backing up against the wall like my very presence is causing her physical pain. It fills her eyes, drowning out her fire. Drowning out the love that shone there only moments ago. In a broken voice, she says, "Why do you keep saving me for a world where you don't exist?"

I rise to meet her, grabbing her shoulders, refusing to let her succumb to this. To become another victim, however indirectly, of Verrick of Wintermoon. "I'm saving you for a world where *you* exist. Where you're free to become the woman you were meant to be. To live the life that was nearly stolen from you time and again. I'm saving you for a world where other people—humans and supernaturals alike—can experience the blessing of having you as a friend, as a partner, as a witch. I'm saving you because when all of us are gone from this world, I want to know that we left it a better place—a place with you in it. Healthy, happy, and alive to feel the sun on your face."

She shakes her head, shoving me away. "No, Draegan. You're pissed at me because I brought them happiness? Goddess, what do you think you all brought me? For the first time in my life, I have people who care about me. People who have my back. True friends and confidants who aren't using me in some sick power game. Lovers who make me feel things I didn't even know I could feel. Could want. Men—*gargoyles* I've come to care for and trust and rely on. And you're telling me it's all a lie?"

"Not a lie, no." I try to smile, but the very act pains me as much as all the things I've had to tell her tonight. "Just... just a truth with an expiration date."

"Fuck off." She swipes at her tears, her cheeks dark and splotchy, her eyes bright. Her fire is back, and now her skin is glowing, too—that ethereal violet light, mesmerizing and beautiful. "There *has* to be a way. Give up on yourself if you want, but *I'm* not giving up on you."

All I want to do is touch her again. Feel that light on my skin. Memorize the curve of her jaw with my fingertips, the soft slope of her neck, the delicate jut of her collarbone...

I sigh. "You know better than most the inherent danger that comes from believing in miracles."

"You bet your ass I do. Yet I believe in them anyway, because a flock of birds once saved me from death in an abandoned subway station, and one night, when I thought my life was finally over for good, I made a wish at the top of a bell tower and a statue turned into a man before my eyes, and that man turned into a gargoyle, and that gargoyle not only saved my life, but made me feel like I could actually be happy again."

"Denial isn't a solution," I snap. Anger and regret and heartbreak wrestle for dominance inside me, the words spilling unbidden. "The others may wish to lose themselves in the land of make-believe with you, but that will not save them any more than a miracle spell that may not even exist. So no, I will *not* be joining you for more family dinners, or for a romp before the fireplace. I will not be feeding you sliced apples at midnight, or carving you pretty things out of ugly bones, or painting your lovely toes the color of the sunset, or gazing into those eyes or caressing your flawless skin or kissing that ripe, red mouth because even being *near* you for more than a moment flays my fucking heart for all the things I want but can *never* have. I don't know how else to say it, Westlyn. But this... Whatever happened between us, whatever you're feeling... It can't go on."

Tears spill from her eyes, but she shakes her head and steps toward me, still refusing to listen. Refusing to budge.

"You trusted me enough to share this with me..." She

takes my hands, gently placing the heart-shaped stone in my palm, her fingers small and delicate against my massive claws. "So trust in this, too. We *will* find a way to break the curse—whatever it takes."

I want to nod. I want to accept her courage, her conviction. I try like hell to hold on to it, to hold her gaze, but all I can see now, all I can hear, all I can *feel* is Verrick of Wintermoon's boot on the back of my neck, my face half in the mud as he ordered his men to kill the people I once held dear...

"You deserved to know about the curse," I say softly. "About our history. But as for a promise of a future... I can't, Westlyn. I'm so sorry, love. But I just can't."

And with that, I turn my back on her and walk away, closing the door behind me.

I tell myself it's for the best. That she's better off. That whatever connection I feel to her is too fleeting to further acknowledge and too complicated to even consider.

And it *is* for the best. I know it, as surely as I've ever known anything.

So why the fuck is there a hole in my chest the size of the damn Chrysler Building?

CHAPTER TWENTY-TWO

DRAEGAN

"Breaking our girl's heart twice in one night?" Jude steps out of the shadows like a ghost, damn near scaring the shit out of me. "Might be a new record."

Fuck. I have no idea how long he's been out here. How much he heard.

But at this particular moment, I can't be bothered to care.

Ignoring him, I head for my suite, eager to lock myself away until it's time to retire on the roof and put this whole fucking night behind me.

But of course he won't let it go. The bastard follows me right into my room.

"Fucking *Jude.*" I whirl on him. "What now? Have you run out of skulls to bludgeon? Would you like mine? Be my fucking guest—just don't spill any blood on my carpet."

Ignoring my rant, he closes my door with a soft click

and leans back against it, arms folded across his chest. "You can't keep running off like this, Drae. Dodging her just because you can't deal with your feelings. You ever think about how *she* feels? What you're doing to her?"

I try to hold on to my anger—Jude's usually a good target for it. But in this case, he's right, and I don't have the strength to die on this hill tonight. "I don't mean to hurt her, Jude. You have to believe that."

"And yet..."

I don't respond. Nothing to say, even though he keeps on staring at me like he's waiting for me to have some kind of epiphany.

The seconds tick by in uncomfortable silence.

I pace.

He remains motionless.

I pace some more.

"Jude, it's not—"

"Bloody hell, Draegan," he finally snaps. "You think I don't know it, mate? You think I don't look at her and see the end of days in her eyes? For fuck's sake. Every one of her precious heartbeats is like a death knell counting down to our eternal darkness."

"Then how can you stand there and ask me why I keep walking away from her? How come *you're* not walking away?"

"Because I'm in love with her, arsehole."

I scoff. "Then you're a damned fool."

"Fine. Then I'm a fool, Draegan. A damned fool who

blatantly ignores everything smart and right his head is saying to him." He jabs a finger hard into my chest. "So what do you call a man who ignores his own fucking *heart*? A man who'd rather lock himself in a room inside his own skull with no windows, no light, no chance of escape, all because his head tells him it's the right thing to do? A man who ignores what's right in front of him because—"

"Because we're going to leave her behind!" I roar. "We could be ripped from this existence at any moment, Jude! How do you think she'd feel then?"

"You don't know how long we've got before—"

"A year? Still not enough. Months? It could be five fucking days for all we—"

"And I'd rather have five fucking days with her and all of you—our fucking *family*—then a thousand more years without her. A thousand more hours, if that's all we've got left. It doesn't matter, Draegan. Can't you see that? A day or a century... Life is too short to spend it brooding in the shadows and cursing the fates. We've already dealt with more than our fair share of shadows and curses. Now? I want the fucking fairy tale, even if I only get it for a little while."

"She still thinks there's a chance of breaking our curse. After everything I explained to her tonight, she's still holding on to some blind hope."

"And what's wrong with hope?"

"You know what breaking the curse means for us! We won't survive it. Not a chance. And even if we did, what then? She's mortal, Jude. She's got a long life ahead of her, yes. But not an immortal one. One way or the other, we will all be parted from her. So what's the bloody point?"

He shakes his head, his jaw ticking. After an agonizingly long beat, he says, "She's not mortal, Draegan."

"Don't be ridiculous. For all intents and purposes, witches are as mortal as mundane humans."

"She's not just a witch. She's dark fae."

"Yes, we already know she's got a bit of it in her bloodline, but that's not enough to—"

"Not a bit. *Half*. Half fae means she's not a mortal. No, maybe not completely immortal, but she's got a *much* longer life ahead of her than a human."

I blink at him, certain I misheard. "But... her mother was a witch. And her father—"

"Is not the mage Brian Avery. Rook cracked the SSD card—it's full of her mother's diaries."

"What are you saying?"

"Westlyn Avery," he continues, "is the child of Madison Strauss and some bloody dark fae noble who tricked the woman into falling in love with him. Once she figured out his true nature, she escaped—barely—but apparently the monster haunted her in dreams, swearing he'd one day hunt down his child, reclaim her in the name of his court, and steal her out of the human realm for good."

The words cut through me like daggers.

Dark fae. Hunt her down. Noble. Court. Steal.

I can barely speak through the fear lodged in my throat, but somehow, I force the words out anyway. "*Which* court?"

Jude shakes his head, and for the first time since he accosted me in the hallway, I see true fear reflected in his eyes, too. Fathomless. Black. Hopeless.

I already have my answer, but I ask again anyway, my teeth gritted, barely keeping the rage in check. "Which. Court?"

"Wintermoon," he finally says, confirming my worst nightmare. "Her father is a noble of Wintermoon, Drae. Serving in the King's court with the rest of the high born dickheads."

"She doesn't know?"

"She will soon enough. Rook's going to give her the diaries tonight. Sent me up here to fetch you both."

I close my eyes, my heart thudding loud in my ears.

The Wintermoon nobles have always been notoriously possessive bastards. Land, magic, women, babies—it's all the same to them. All things to conquer and possess in the name of King Verrick.

Our past has finally caught up with us, all the threads of our lives tangled in knots we can never escape.

"The rune on the back of her neck," I say, the sudden realization chilling me to the marrow. "It's not a binding rune, Jude. It's a fucking tracking device."

CHAPTER TWENTY-THREE

WESTLYN

My head is spinning from everything Draegan shared about their curse, about his family. From holding him in my arms as he bared his soul for the first time since his life was ripped apart. From feeling his hot tears on my skin as he wept for a family he never got to mourn.

And then... feeling the walls rise once again around his heart, completely shutting me out.

The scent of him lingers in the air, making my blood boil.

Damn it, Draegan.

My heart is broken for him. I can't draw a single breath without feeling his pain.

But I'm also *royally* pissed off. I'm damn near vibrating with it.

No chance at surviving the curse? Fuck that.

You will *survive the curse, Draegan Caldwell. I'll make damn sure of that. It's* me *you might not survive.*

Ditching my shorts, I pull on a warmer pair of sweatpants and fuzzy slippers, grab the fae amulet stone from my night table, then head downstairs, determined to lock myself in the library for as long as it takes to finish transcribing the Codex.

The amulet pulses in my hand, and I smile. Good. That fucking curse doesn't stand a chance against me.

But the moment I pass the study, I know right away something is wrong.

Seated on the sofa with a drink in one hand and his tablet in the other, Rook looks exhausted. His eyes are red, shoulders stiff, knee bouncing in an uncharacteristic show of nerves.

Auggie's pacing before the fire, his hazel eyes wide and unfocused.

"What happened?" I gasp.

They both startle, which is another red flag—they can always hear and scent me coming.

My heart lodges in my throat. "Guys? Is everything—"

Movement behind me. Warm hands sliding around my stomach, a comforting nuzzle against my neck. The scent of candle flame and black pepper. *Jude.*

"Let's sit, scarecrow," he whispers into my hair. "Rook's got some news."

Draegan's with him, too, his face grim. He briefly meets

my gaze, then quickly looks away, heading past me toward the bar. But even in that brief instant, I saw it.

Not regret about our argument. Not anger over my refusal to listen to his version of "reason."

But fear.

Swallowing hard, I allow Jude to lead me into the study, and I take a seat on the sofa next to Rook. His wing comes around behind my shoulder.

A drink is thrust in front of me, and when I glance up, I find Draegan holding the glass.

"You may want this," he says. The scent of expensive cognac wafts up.

I take a few sips, steadying myself.

"We got into the files," Rook says softly. "The SSD card."

Another sip. A deep, shuddering breath. "Tell me," I whisper.

They all exchange a loaded glance.

Rook hands me his tablet, his honey eyes full of compassion. "Your mother left you letters, West. Diaries of some sort. All written to you while she was pregnant. I didn't read all of them—just a few as I was transferring the files. I wanted you to decide what to share or keep private."

"Letters? From... from my mom?" Tears well in my eyes, and I can't help the smile that spreads across my face, or the nervous laugh that follows it. "Goddess! I thought someone died, or Eloise had found a way to get to me, or... You're all looking at me like I've got an expiration date. But my mother left me letters? A chance to get to know her in a way I never could before? This is... this..."

I trail off, realizing none of them have returned my laugh. They're all still looking at me like the bomb is about to drop.

"West, before you read them..." Rook's hand is warm on my thigh. Across from us, Jude watches me carefully. Auggie's still pacing, and Draegan... He's in the corner nursing a drink, his jaw tight, wings stiff with tension. "I'm going to tell you this one thing," Rook continues. "The most important thing."

I nod, heart hammering in my chest.

He blows out a deep breath, then says, "Brian Avery is not your biological father."

"He... *what?*"

"Your father is... At least, according to your mother... He's a—"

"Your *father*," Draegan says, unable to keep the vitriol from his tone, "is a dark fae noble of the Wintermoon court. And he'll never stop hunting you."

Icy dread slithers down my spine and wraps around my heart.

Wintermoon. The same cutthroat fae who cursed the men I love.

"Subtle, Drae," Auggie says. "Real subtle."

"For fuck's sake," Draegan snaps. "She doesn't need subtle. She needs the truth."

Auggie slams his glass down on the mantle. "She needs

time to process—"

"No, Draegan's right," I say softly. "I need the truth, as painful and terrifying as it's going to be. All of it. No sugar-coating, no subtleties."

The gargoyles nod.

I take a deep, steadying breath.

Down the rest of the drink.

And with Rook's tablet in my lap and my fae amulet clutched tight, I read the first words my mother has ever given me.

My dearest daughter,

I have only just learned of your existence, and I'm already hopelessly in love with you. I'm writing these letters to you—dairies, if you will—for many reasons. A gift to my beloved daughter, so that you may know how much you mean to me. A record of all that led to your creation, so you may understand your legacy. And, most importantly, a warning.

You are in grave danger, my love.

I don't know when you'll see these letters—how old you'll be, where you'll be living, what horrors you might've already endured. But if you're reading them, it means the worst has indeed happened. It means I'm gone from your life. It means Brian is also gone—taken from you by death or some other nefarious force, for he would never leave you willingly. You must believe that above all else. Brian Avery fell in love with you the moment I told him about you, just as I did.

I only wish I could love him the way he loves me. The way he's always loved me. But for that, I'm grateful. It means he will care for you as his own, even though you were created by another man.

I am filled with regret to know that this is how you are finding out, but again, if you're reading these letters, all of our safeguards have failed.

The man who fathered you isn't a man at all. He's fae. A high born dark fae of the Wintermoon court. That name is likely insignificant to you—in fact, I pray that it is, for that means you've yet to encounter the fae from your father's realm. His people.

I will explain everything to you, my love. So perhaps these letters are more than just a gift, a record, and a warning.

Perhaps they are a confession. I beg your forgiveness.

Your devoted mother,

Madison

CHAPTER TWENTY-FOUR

WESTLYN

I read the first letter several times, the gargoyles silent, the crackling flames in the fireplace the only soundtrack to the revelation that will forever separate my life into "before" and "after."

Before, I was a magicless daughter of a powerful witch who died during childbirth and a mage who never really wanted me.

After—*now*—I'm a half-witch, half-fae hybrid with magic I'm only just beginning to experience, and a legacy that—if my mother is speaking the truth—has put me in even more danger than the shadow magic society and the demon prince.

Gathering my courage, I take another breath and scroll to the next letter. I try to stay focused on the words, to read them slowly and carefully, but soon my eyes are moving faster than my brain can absorb anything, my mind eager to uncover my mother's secrets. *My* secrets.

"She was experimenting with fae magic," I say, still skimming. "Somehow she became trapped in the fae realm. A Wintermoon female befriended her, inviting her to court."

"It's how they entice mortals," Draegan says. "An offer of friendship, a chance to see another world. To indulge in all the majestic wonders of the fae courts. But when it comes to the fae, there are *always* strings attached."

I nod, reading on. "She met—him," I say, unable to call him my father, "at a royal masquerade ball the female friend invited her to. He was attending with some of the other nobles, dressed in black and violet silks, wearing a golden mask."

Her words paint the picture of a story I know all too well—a fairy tale beginning.

From the moment I laid eyes on him, there was no one else in that ballroom. Tall and sinewy, with hair the color of the darkest night and eyes like burnished silver. Even through the mask, his eyes entranced me. He asked me to honor him with a dance, but I was the one who was honored.

We waltzed for hours. Days, it seemed, his eyes holding me in his thrall, his laughter like a drug, his scent equally intoxicating. By the time the music faded, I was already in love with him.

We created you that very night, my love. Under the fae moon and more glittering stars than you will ever see in the human realm.

I skim through the overly poetic description of how I

came into being. Not because I can't handle the idea of my mother having sex, but because the longer she goes on, it's so clear to me—an outsider looking in on a rose-colored memory—how manipulative he was, how deceptive.

She's a tiny rabbit in a snare, and he's nothing more than a wolf toying with his meal.

I tell the guys about the ball, the way the night ended.

"But after a few more nights," I say, "it sounds like he wanted her to return home."

At first, I didn't want to leave, my mother writes. *But he insisted I must, promising me he would call for me again—that I could return to him soon. Trusting this, I returned home.*

Home to Brian.

I thought I'd spent a few nights in Wintermoon, dancing and laughing, falling in love, making love under a blanket of stars night after night... Imagine my surprise when Brian told me I'd been gone for months. I felt as though I had lost all touch with reality. He was out of his mind with worry.

As the days passed, I began to doubt my fae lover. His intentions. His words. The very words that had so thoroughly entranced me were now poisoning my mind. My heart.

I realized that he'd lied to me. Used me. That he would only do so again, and through my confession I promised Brian I would never return to the fae realm. To my Wintermoon noble.

Alas, it wasn't long after that I learned of you. And I knew in that instant I could never love anything more, regardless of your parentage or how you came to me. You were and are a blessing...

I skim through a few more entries, each one growing increasingly dark.

He knows, my sweet girl. I don't know if he's got spies on me, or if this was his plan all along—to leave me with child in hopes of one day claiming you as his own, another subject for the royal court, another witch to do his bidding. But he knows about you. He knows I've got you, knows how much I love you, and he will use that to manipulate me...

And another, a few nights later:

He's haunting my dreams, turning them into nightmares. It's the only way he can reach me, for he's not strong enough to come to our realm. He promises me the world, and I know his words are poison, yet...

Again, the letters take a turn, oscillating between revulsion and obsession.

He came to me again last night, she writes. *His voice like liquid silk, his touch like fire. I know I should resist him, but my resolve is weakening. He asks about you. He has always wanted a daughter, he says. A female heir to his fae lands, his immeasurable wealth, his magic. He assures me he will spoil you. When I refuse his invitations, he becomes nothing but darkness and flame. Even in dreams, his temper is destructive. And yet, he is shockingly beautiful. I wonder if you will inherit his eyes...*

The entries only become more cryptic and strange, alternating between declarations of her borderline obsessive love for my fae father and her paralyzing fear of him. Fear for herself, yes. But mostly, fear for me.

He'll never stop hunting you, she writes—the same exact

phrase Draegan used. Not searching for you, not reaching out to you, but *hunting* you. *He will use every bit of power and connection and influence he has to find a way into this realm or to bring you to his. It may take days, it may take years, but mark my words, he will find you...*

"I can't," I finally say, turning off the tablet. "I can't read any more tonight. It's all just... it's too much."

Rook's wing draws closer, and I lean into his touch, steadying myself with his calming presence.

"Brian Avery wasn't my real father," I whisper, the revelation washing over me again like a dark wave. "And he knew. Goddess, no wonder he tried to sell me off to a demon. He probably resented me. Probably looked at me and saw nothing but a big neon sign reminding him of my mother's affair."

My mother's affair.

The words sound so preposterous, I almost laugh.

For my entire life, I've only ever known her as a ghost. A woman who died giving birth to me, frozen in my mind as wholly perfect simply because she didn't live long enough to hurt or disappoint me.

But she wasn't perfect. She was as flawed and broken as any of us.

I know it's irrational to judge her for it. I didn't know her, didn't know her relationship with my—with Brian. Didn't know what would make her fall in obsessive love with a fae noble from an evil court, unable to see through his manipulations.

But for some reason, the proof of her flaws—written in her own words, a shockingly intimate tale—breaks my heart anyway.

I wanted her to be above reproach. Not just in my mind, but in life.

"My father is... Wintermoon," I say. Another dark wave. Another icy chill. Even at a whisper, the word makes the hairs on my neck stand on end, skin prickling where the rune is undoubtedly glowing. "My rune... Do you think my biological father marked me? Or his magic did, somehow? Like it just knew I was... Wintermoon?"

"Another drink?" Draegan asks, taking my empty glass. When I shake my head, he says, "Yes. I'm concerned the rune might be a sort of... A way for the fae to find you."

"A tracking device?"

He nods. "The Wintermoon fae... They're possessive and cruel, Miss Avery. When I said they would hunt you, I wasn't exaggerating. The noble knew about you from the start—he's very likely been tracking you ever since. I'm sure it's only by the grace of the failing portals that he hasn't come for you. Your mother mentioned he wasn't able to travel here, and it's certainly only gotten more difficult for him in recent years. That's a good thing for us, but we can't rely on that alone."

"If he's anything like his kin," Jude says, and I can't recall a time when I've ever seen him so pale. Not even when I first told him about the mages who carved my back. "He's relentless and bloodthirsty. He'll stop at nothing to try to take you—emphasis on *try*. Because if I catch so much as a *whiff* of Wintermoon blood..." The color returns to his cheeks, fire rising beneath his gray skin.

"It's important that you're aware of all of this," Draegan says to me. "And you must be vigilant. But it's not for you to lose sleep over it. We *will* take care of this." And then, kneeling before me, a rare moment of vulnerability in his eyes, "We will take care of *you*. Always."

He reaches for my hand, and I let him take it. Let him fold his giant fingers around mine. He leans forward, pressing warm, soft lips to my forehead.

"Always," he repeats.

And despite all the confusion and tension and hurt still lingering between us, I know he speaks the truth.

CHAPTER TWENTY-FIVE

AUGUSTINE

After the revelation about West's biological father, we're all in agreement.

All threats against Westlyn are to be eliminated without hesitation. We no longer have the luxury of presuming innocence or waiting for that elusive thing called proof. Though we've yet to completely piece together the links between the shadow magic society, Zorakkov, and now the Wintermoon fae, we're operating under the assumption that they're *all* working together toward a single end.

Westlyn.

Whether they mean to kill her, to bind her to a demon prince, to send her back to the fae realm, or to use her in some other yet-to-be-revealed scheme... Who gives a fuck? Rook's working every angle he can to try to find those answers, but the rest of us? We don't need to know the grand plans to know that *none* of them will come to fruition.

As long as we're here to protect her, no one will so much as *breathe* on a single hair on her precious head.

"You ready to do this?" I ask Draegan.

It's the night after we learned about West's dark fae father, and now, high above Lexington Avenue, Drae and I are perched outside the fiftieth-floor conference room of the Bank of New Amsterdam's main building.

The offices are mostly empty at this late hour, but across the hall from the conference room, a soft golden light spills out from beneath a closed door.

The office of Kevin Klaiburn.

The old man's burning the midnight oil. Likely running his after-hours smut club enterprise away from the prying eyes of his underlings.

It's too bad we have to ice him. I rather enjoyed collecting his dossier over the years. Lots of entertaining stuff in there.

Draegan gives me a curt nod.

"What's the play?" I ask.

"Question him. Then end it clean. Make it look like a robbery—a gift for our friends at the station."

"You sure you don't want to bring Jude in on this?"

Drae shakes his head. "We don't need to torture the old man. We just need him to cease to exist."

"Deleting people from existence is Jude's specialty."

"Yes, but deleting them quickly is not. No games tonight, Augustine. No long and bloody goodbyes and artistic souvenirs. We're getting whatever information he's willing to offer under threat of death, then we're executing that threat. I don't have the stomach for anything else tonight."

"Same page, brother. Same page."

Jude's antics are often necessary and occasionally amusing, but when it comes to eliminating the lingering threats against Westlyn? The quicker the better, as far as I'm concerned.

"You worried about fallout with Reedsy?" I ask. "And whoever else he's got lined up to press us about that judge?"

"Always a risk, but it's clear now he's not investigating Westlyn as a missing person—never was. He knew she was in that wreck. He tracked her like a fucking animal and made the call that nearly got her captured, all at Lennon Forsythe's behest. And it happened after our bank visit—a visit only Klaiburn was supposed to know about. They're *all* in bed together."

When we first learned that Drae and West had been followed after leaving the bank, we suspected Klaiburn's involvement, but Drae wanted to wait for more proof. Wanted a chance to sniff around, see if we could unearth any of the other little moles on Forsythe's payroll.

But with the new intel on West's lineage, that's not happening now.

Like I said, proof is a luxury we can no longer afford. Hell, maybe we never could.

Clear on the plan, Drae and I sail up to the roof and enter through the fire exit, then pull up our human glamours. Thanks to one of Rook's handy devices, we're able to temporarily disable the alarms and dodge the surprisingly few interior cameras, quickly making our way down to the fiftieth floor.

There's no kicking down doors, guns blazing. No explosives or otherwise grand entrances.

Drae simply turns the doorknob to Klaiburn's office, and in we walk.

The old man practically leaps from his chair like a kid caught jerking off to porn in his father's study, but the moment he recognizes us, he drops right back down again, cursing under his breath.

To his credit, the old man doesn't play stupid.

He knows why we're here.

"I didn't have a choice, Caldwell," he mutters. "You've got very, very powerful enemies."

"We have that in common, then," Drae replies. "Do you have any idea what sort of line you've crossed?"

"I had to pick a side."

"You picked wrong."

Klaiburn nods, acceptance settling into his eyes. If he's frightened, he doesn't show it. I wonder if he's even the tiniest bit relieved.

For a man with as many shameful secrets as Klaiburn, death is often the best exit plan.

Drae takes the chair across from him. I remain in the

doorway keeping watch, though I doubt Klaiburn's going to bother with a silent alarm. He'll be dead before help arrives, anyway.

Setting his gun and attached silencer on the desk, Drae says, "In deference to our long years of association, I'm hoping you'll be willing to answer a few questions."

"Shoot," he says, and then laughs. I can't help but return it. Even Drae cracks a smile at that.

"Do you know where Lennon and Celine Forsythe are hiding?" Drae asks.

"No," Klaiburn replies. "Only that they *are* hiding. Not long after the fire, they went off-grid. Everything that's happened since was coordinated through anonymous sources within the society."

"What about Detective Grant Reedsy?" Drae asks.

"As far as I know, he's out of the country. Somewhere in South America by now, I believe. That was his plan after the—"

"*Don't*," Drae practically growls. "Do not mention the events of that night to me if you value the lives of your family members."

At this, Klaiburn pales. Then, a quick nod. "As far as I know, Reedsy got on a plane a few nights ago."

"What can you tell us about the shadow magic society's involvement with the dark fae?" Drae asks, and we both watch Klaiburn closely. This is the first time we've ever directly mentioned anything supernatural to him by name.

The last of the light drains from his eyes.

"I don't like to speak of the dark fae," he says. "No disrespect to your kind, Caldwell, but some of your kin make *you* seem downright pleasant."

"They are no kin of mine, I assure you."

"Regardless... I've only had the displeasure of dealing with them directly on a handful of occasions, and they certainly never shared anything significant with me. The few of their kind who've been able to travel here were mostly interested in my... other business operations."

"Why does that not surprise me?" I roll my eyes. Dark fae trolling high-end sex clubs for mortal pussy? Sounds like the pitch for a terrible TV series.

"They seem to be involved in some kind of dealings with Forsythe's son," he continues. "Though I can't say what. Hunter Forsythe is even cagier than his parents. I rarely spoke with the boy."

Drae and I scrutinize him. It doesn't seem like he knows Hunter's a demon—rather, a vessel for one.

I also don't get the sense he knows anything useful at all.

Klaiburn must come to the same conclusion. I can see it in his eyes. The realization that these will be his final moments.

With a deep sigh, he points at the back of the door where a dark gray suit jacket hangs. "Pass me that jacket, if you don't mind."

I yank it off the hook, give it a thorough search, then toss it at him. He stands and puts it on. Straightens his tie.

Removes his wedding band and watch, wallet, phone, keys. Sits back down and smooths back his white hair.

"I suppose you're going to kill me now," he says plainly.

Draegan nods—a single, solemn thing—and for the first time in all these long millennia, I see the burden he carries.

For Draegan, there is no pleasure in killing. None of Jude's sick fascination. None of the adrenaline rush I usually feel, or Rook's morbid curiosity about a man's final words.

Draegan kills because he must. Just like he did when we were humans fighting for our homeland. Our friends.

That war against Wintermoon... All the things we lost... Fuck, it changed us all in so many ways.

But at his core, Draegan is and will always remain good. Will always have that innate sense of right and wrong that first drove him to fight for us, to lead us onto those bloody battlefields, to offer himself up to the dark fae king who would only ever seek to manipulate and hurt.

It's the same sense of right and wrong that drives him to protect Westlyn even as he resists the deeper connection I know he feels.

The love.

Draegan wraps his hand around the gun. Takes aim.

I reach for my phone. Pull up the camera. Focus.

I don't know why I compose the shot. Perhaps it's because this rare glimpse of Drae's humanity gives me hope that some indelible part of us still lives. Perhaps I need the reminder that the four of us *were* human once, and that somewhere deep down—beneath the glamours we were forced to adopt to hide the gargoyles we were forced to become—we still are.

"For Westlyn Avery," Drae whispers.

"For Westlyn Avery," I repeat.

I click the shutter button.

Snap.

Draegan pulls the trigger.

Bang.

Blood and brains splatter the wall, and Drae and I watch in silence for a long moment as the gore slides down in dark rivulets, soaking into the edge of the carpet. It matches Klaiburn's suit coat, I realize. Dark gray. The carpet, the suit, the walls, his eyes.

Wordlessly, we gather up the valuables Klaiburn left on the desk, along with a laptop and tablet, leaving the bulkier desktop computer behind.

We also take a couple of small external hard drives, a box of thumb drives from the desk drawer, and two file boxes filled with old-school handwritten ledgers.

When the detectives sent to investigate the murder discover the missing files, they'll know whoever did this knew about Klaiburn's shady dealings. Most of them are on the take, their bosses members of the clubs. The missing files will send a clear message.

Push this too far, and your skeletons will be revealed as well.

The missing property—the valuable stuff—will give them an easy out.

Robbery gone bad. Case closed. Locks on closet doors intact, keeping those skeletons at bay.

For now.

CHAPTER TWENTY-SIX

WESTLYN

Another nightmare. Another night waking up with the sunset to find myself drenched in sweat, the claws of dark dream-enemies slowly receding.

I dreamed of the fire again, of flames spilling from a great cauldron like the one in the Judgment card, devouring the city, its buildings, its people. This time, I was chained to Zorakkov by a collar around my neck, and all the while, the mysterious dark fae monster whispered through my memories, his cold rasp an echo in my skull...

Don't fear, little one. Everything is unfolding exactly as it should be...

I kick off the sheets and take a few deep breaths, clearing the wreckage from my mind—more fallout from my mother's truth bombs, no doubt. Over the past three nights, I've read through her letters dozens of times, only to end up more confused than ever.

And more determined to figure out my magic. Dark fae or not, I need to get a better handle on it... Before *it* gets a handle on me.

The guys keep reassuring me that just because my father is a Wintermoon fae doesn't mean I've inherited his evil. That at the end of the day, we all have choices, and bad genetics aren't a death sentence. But we're not talking about *human* genetics. I've got noble fae blood running through my veins. *Dark* fae blood. And not just any dark fae, but the worst of the worst.

The runes, the glowing violet light, the magic that allows me to read the Codex...

Until I can figure out exactly what it is, exactly where it comes from, and exactly what it can do, I'm not making any assumptions.

They tell me I'm good because they *want* me to be good. That's who they see when they look at me. Hell, that's who *I* see when I look at myself. But I spent too many years of my life being too scared and submissive to look beneath the surface. I can't do that anymore—not with this.

My gargoyles are too important to me.

I sit up in bed—Jude's bed, if we're being technical—and stretch my arms over my head, popping my back. Huxley pads into the room, followed by his sister, undoubtedly looking for snacks.

"Did you two already eat your hidden stash of crackers?" I laugh, giving them both head rubs and a few kisses before

I spot a gift box on the night table with an envelope addressed to me.

I recognize Rook's handwriting immediately.

Stomach fizzing with delight, I tear open the envelope and read the card.

Gone out to Long Island to meet with my occult studies contact tonight. I'll be back late. In the meantime, here's a little something to help ensure you're safe, and a little something else to help ensure I'm never far from your thoughts... among other things.

Fondly,
Your Naughty Professor,
Rook

On that deliciously mysterious note, I set the card aside and open the box, revealing two items, each with their own additional card.

The first is a smartwatch customized with a band of pretty silver links.

You can use this to call, text, or video chat with any of us, the card says. *As well as emergency services. As long as you're wearing it, we'll always have a way to get to you. I hope you like the design.*

It's beautiful—the perfect mix of modern and classic. I fasten it around my wrist, surprised at how light it is, and turn it on. The black face comes to life with the time and date.

The second card reads, *I designed this especially for you. It's clean and ready to wear. No further instructions but this: put it in. NOW.*

Put it *in*? Does he mean *on*? Is he still talking about the watch? But... no. This note was definitely attached to the second gift. It's a small silk pouch holding something about the size and shape of a tube of lipstick, but much weightier.

I open the pouch and tip the object into my palm. Smooth, silver, rounded on both ends like a...

Oh, goddess. Is this what I think it is?

The moment the thought enters my mind, the mysterious little bullet starts vibrating in my hand, startling my poor ravens out of the room.

The watch lights up with a video call.

Rook.

I tap it to accept the call. His face immediately fills the screen, and the vibrating stops.

"You aren't wearing your gift," he says by way of a greeting.

"The watch?" I blurt out. "Yes I am! I love it! I'm talking to you on it right now!"

He glares at me. I've never seen him so... so bold. So commanding.

"Put it in, Wild West."

It feels like a scolding, and my cheeks heat. "Wait... You mean now? By myself?"

An eyebrow arches over his glasses. His only response.

A thrill races up my spine, and I lie back in bed,

suddenly eager to follow my naughty professor's every command.

I'm about to put it in when he says suddenly, "*Show* me."

Goddess, I've never done anything like this before.

But I want to. Oh, how I want to be his good little student.

Angling the watch so he can see exactly what I'm doing, I spread my thighs and slide the vibrator in. Immediately, it comes back to life, vibrating until I feel it settle snuggly inside me, then stopping all too soon.

"Rook!" I gasp, bringing the watch up to my face. "We're stopping? No! Why are we stopping?"

His smile is dark and devious, his honey eyes glowing. "Because, my wild girl. I won't be home for hours. I need to ration out your pleasure slowly and methodically."

"But... what?" I bolt upright. "I have to leave it in?"

"It's a wearable device, West. Designed to remain inside you and remind you, at my urging..." It buzzes again, and I gasp as tiny waves of pure ecstasy radiate through my core. But then, all too soon, it stops.

Again.

Argh...

"...that I'm thinking of you," Rook continues.

"How? How are you controlling this thing?"

"Easy." His devious grin turns smug. "I paired it with your smartwatch and hacked it with my phone. Now, be a good girl and leave everything in place, and you'll be *thoroughly* rewarded later."

The promise in his words obliterates my frustration.

Rewarded later...

Goddess, we've been skirting that line for so long, our all-night sessions in the library bringing us closer than ever —shared theories about Zorakkov's end game, about Eloise, about the original Cerridwen witches and the esoteric text of the Codex. Cuddling on the sofa before the fireplace, tucked protectively under his wing as I practice connecting with my magic. Forehead kisses and foot rubs for me, wing and back massages for him.

The kind of sweet, devoted closeness that can otherwise take years to build, but was always so easy with us.

But the other kind of closeness? The searing hot kisses, the tangle of limbs, the touches that leave you gasping and breathless and trembling?

That line remains uncrossed.

Until now.

I'm already imagining the taste of his kiss, the feel of his big hands spreading my thighs, the heat of his mouth as he—

"West," he warns, hitting me with another all-too-brief buzz. "*Behave* yourself. At least until I get home."

"You... You're trying to distract me from my mom's letters," I say. "Since you won't be here tonight to keep me from spiraling, you're—"

The vibrations kick up into high gear, cutting off my words and threatening to destroy me from the inside out in the *best* possible way.

"No, beautiful," he growls, his voice low and dangerous and so fucking sexy he could probably make me come from his words alone. "I'm doing this because I want you desperate, soaked, and fucking *begging* for it when I come home tonight. Oh, and West?"

I'm so shocked to hear this filthy, intoxicatingly commanding side of my sweet professor, I can barely mutter a response. "Y-yeah?"

"Don't even *think* about removing it," he says. "I've got eyes in places you can't even imagine."

The screen goes dead, but everything inside me is a live wire.

I close my eyes and wait for him to send another vibration through me, but nothing happens. I wriggle on the bed. Tap the watch face. But Rook is clearly up to no good.

Still. My whole body is now tingling in anticipation of what's to come.

Jude and Auggie are in meetings tonight, but I have no idea where Draegan is. I haven't seen him since the night Rook gave me the letters, which is probably for the best.

I know he's doing what he can to keep me safe. But I have no idea where we stand otherwise.

So, hoping to avoid a run-in, I make quick work of getting dressed and head to the kitchen to pack up a few snacks for the library, which is where I'm planning to spend the hours until Rook returns.

I'm just dishing up the last of Auggie's caramel apple streusel into a takeout container when the silver bullet inside me goes from zero to a hundred in less than a heartbeat, radiating warm waves of shear pleasure throughout my body, setting my nerves on fire.

My clit throbs with need, my pussy clenching around the toy, my knees buckling as I grip the edge of the counter and suck in a breath and chase the release that's so, so close...

Right there, Rook. Don't stop. Don't—

"Miss Avery? What's wrong?"

Draegan.

Fuck.

He's at my side in a flash, gripping my elbows and helping me stand upright again.

Without warning, the vibrator stops.

Damn it!

"Are you hurt? Did something happen? Did you faint?" Draegan's incessant questions only serve to throw more ice water on my dreams for an epic, long-distance orgasm.

"Hi! I'm fine!" My voice is entirely too high and tight, but I force a smile, carefully extracting myself from his grasp and turning to the fridge, wishing I could crawl inside. I grab a bottle of fresh-pressed apple juice and chug it until my heart rate finally returns to normal.

When I look at Draegan again, he's still watching me like a damn hawk.

"You're flushed," he says.

"Just a... hot flash. Womanly things. You don't want to know."

He arches a dubious brow, but I press on.

"Anyway, how are you? Everything good?"

"I'm... I just..." He runs a hand through his salt-and-pepper hair and sighs. "I wanted to let you know that Kevin Klaiburn is no longer a threat. I meant to tell you sooner, but it seems we've been passing ships these past few nights."

I nod, not sure what to say to that.

We may be passing ships, but he's never far from my thoughts. From my heart.

Oh, Draegan. Why won't you let me in?

"We're still searching for Reedsy and the Forsythes," he continues. "That's our top priority. Before his demise, Klaiburn indicated they were in hiding, Reedsy having fled the country. All indications are that Klaiburn was telling the truth. We've got a woman in customs keeping an eye out, ready to alert us the minute he sets foot back on American soil."

"Do you think he will?" I ask. "What if he stays away for good?"

"He's got a wife and children here. At some point, he'll either return or send word for them. We're watching the house, as well as the homes of all his known associates—his partners on the force, his favorite bars, his drug dealer."

"Sounds like you've got all the bases cov—*ohmygoodness*!"

Another shock to my core, strong enough to steal my breath.

"Miss Avery?" Draegan moves to reach for me, but I

take a step back and shake my head, the buzz fading once more.

"Fine," I pant. "Just another... another hot flash. *Woo*, it's like summer in here, isn't it? Time to bust out the lemonade and—"

No. Not again. Rook!

Draegan cocks his head. "Did you hear that?"

"No! I mean... hear... what?"

"Some sort of... buzzing sound. Only, muffled." He takes a step toward me, his gray eyes scrutinizing my face. "There! There it is again. It seems to be coming from—"

"Hungry!" I blurt out, my legs quaking now, sweat beading on the back of my neck, my clit begging for friction and holy shit I'm going to *kill* Rook when he gets home. After he ravishes me, of course, but still. Dead!

"Grumbling stomach!" I explain. "You know how it is. Anyway, thanks for the update, good looking out, keep me posted, bye!"

I grab my container of streusel and bolt for the door, but just before I make it out, Draegan grabs my hand, and I stop.

So does the buzzing.

I'm not sure whether to be annoyed or relieved about that, but the moment I turn around and catch Draegan's gaze—wild and tempestuous, full of emotion—I decide I'm relieved.

"Draegan," I whisper, my heart cracking open for him all over again. "I don't—"

"I never should've let them live as long as I did," he says, his voice choked with regret. "Reedsy, Lennon, Celine, their staff... All of them. I should've known Reedsy's interest in your case went deeper than his petty grievances with our organization. I should've known Forsythe would find other ways to get to you. I should've—"

"None of that is your fault, and I refuse to let you take that blame." I squeeze his hand. "We're all in this together, okay?"

He stares at me for so long I start to wonder if he even heard me. But then, finally, he nods.

"I'm going out to the library to work on the Codex," I say.

"Again?"

"And again and again until I've cracked every mystery." I smile. "Hey, I told you I'm not stopping until I find a way to free you, and I meant it."

He cups my face, a new storm brewing in his eyes.

"Westlyn," he whispers, stroking my cheek with his thumb, his touch so gentle I close my eyes and lose myself in it, just for a moment. "Sometimes when I look into your eyes, I start to wonder if maybe you already have. If maybe you set us free that very first night we met, and this is merely my soul's version of heaven."

I suck in a sharp breath, his palm so warm against my cheek, my heart thundering...

I feel his soft touch slip away.

And when I finally open my eyes again, he's gone.

CHAPTER TWENTY-SEVEN

ROOK

From the moment the dark fae made us, gargoyles have been legends. Myths. The stuff of nightmares and books, stories told around the fire and—many centuries later—the screen.

That's what the fae intended.

Gargoyles aren't supposed to exist. So we *don't.*

By unspoken agreement, Draegan, Auggie, Jude, and I have kept our dark secret for fifteen hundred years. Aside from Draegan's unintentional reveal to Eloise the night she attacked West, we've only shown our true forms in the rarest of cases—usually, when we're about to send a man to his grave, where he *can't* reveal our secrets.

And then, to Westlyn Avery, on the first night she came to us. Draegan wanted to impress upon her just how dire her circumstances were. Just how much danger she was truly in, with no one to trust but the fierce monsters who'd taken her captive.

But, unbeknownst to my gargoyle brothers, there's another who knows what lurks behind our human glamours.

And it's her council I seek tonight.

"Do you ever wonder whether immortality is *truly* forever?" Tatiana says when she opens her door to greet me. "Surely even *we* cannot outrun time."

I offer a small bow and a big smile, realizing just how much I've missed her. "That doesn't stop us from trying."

"Sometimes..." She draws her shawl close over her bony shoulders and holds out her hand, inspecting the network of veins and spots on the back. "Sometimes I feel as though I'm one of the great standing stones of old, Rook. Slowly eroded by the seductive kiss of an evening breeze. One night, that very breeze will carry the dust of my bones back to the stars."

"But not *this* night, I hope." I offer my arm and escort her back into the house.

In the mundane world, Tatiana is a renowned professor of occult studies. She used to travel around the globe to lecture and teach, but now she works primarily out of NYU. I met her over a century ago, sitting in on one of her lectures on demonic possession. She identified me as supernatural right away, cornered me after class, and demanded to know if I'd ever visited hell.

We've been friends ever since.

In recent years, however, she's grown more reclusive,

only lecturing for special graduate classes and even then, doing most of her work online.

It's been over a decade since I've seen her in person, our communications limited to the occasional text or email puzzling out one occult theory or another, and now she looks more frail than I remember.

But the vampire-witch is even older than we are, and will almost certainly outlast us all.

In the kitchen, she puts on water for tea and sets out a plate of lemon cookies dusted with powdered sugar.

Then, gesturing for me to drop the human glamor, she settles in across from me at her small kitchen table. "Now. What brings your handsome face to my doorstep this evening, old friend?"

"Questions, Tatiana. Always questions."

"Is that all?"

"To be perfectly honest, I could also use a stronger perimeter spell, if you're up for it." I pop a cookie into my mouth, the powdered sugar coating my lips. "I'm concerned mine aren't up to the task."

She arches a delicate silver brow. "To protect something in, or to keep something out?"

"To protect something precious that's *in*, and to keep all who seek to harm that something precious *out*."

"Very well." She's on her feet again. "I'll pour the tea, then we shall brew your spell and answer all your questions. But first, you must answer one of mine."

"Anything."

A smile twitches her lips. "What's her name?"

I remove my glasses and polish them with one of her cloth napkins, my cheeks heating. "Sorry. Whose name?"

"Don't be coy with me, Rook Van Doren." She cups my jaw, peering into my face. "The woman who put the light back into those soulful brown eyes of yours. I want to know *all* about her."

Sipping my lavender-vanilla tea, I tell Tatiana only enough to satisfy her mother-hen curiosity.

Not West's name, or the fact that she's essentially a fugitive in hiding from the Archmage and all the vile shadow magic bastards under his command.

Not her recently discovered fae lineage, or her ability to tap into a strange magic we've yet to identify, or the fact that she's the one with the rune on her neck in the photos I've shared.

It's clear that I'm being guarded, but Tatiana doesn't push.

She never does. Just lets me come to things in my own time, like any good professor should.

While she gathers the ingredients for the perimeter spell, I chance a quick peek at my phone, checking the security feed for the library.

My witch is curled up on the sofa with the Codex, diligently transcribing.

Every few minutes, I tap my phone, sending her a little jolt. The sight of her pink cheeks and squirming body is enough to bolster me through the long night ahead.

Still thinking of you, Wild West, I text her now.

I wish I could tell you you're the worst, she replies via her watch, *but I love every horrible thing you're doing to me, Professor.*

Stifling a chuckle, I text back, *Nothing will prepare you for the horrible things I'm going to do to you the moment I return to Blackmoor.*

At this, she glances up at one of the security cameras and flips me off.

"The spell needs to simmer a bit," Tatiana says, gesturing for me to bring the tea and cookies and follow her into her home office. "Let's get to those questions. Is this about the rune?"

I nod. "And some other things that may or may not be related. Have you had a chance to look at the new images I sent? Do you still think it's a binding rune?"

"Yes and no."

"What do you mean?" I move a pile of old tomes out of the way and take a seat in a worn leather chair beside her desk.

She hands me her tablet, one of Auggie's photos on the screen—a closeup of West's rune. "This appears to be the dark fae rune that loosely translates to the word 'kept,' but can have different meanings and uses related to that word. Such as... kept out, or kept safe. Much like your perimeter spell." She smiles. "You can see how such a symbol could be used as a binding rune—to *keep* one's inherent magic at bay, or to *keep* one from accessing it, for example."

"I assumed that's what we were dealing with. A magical lock box, so to speak."

"Yes. However, the second set of images you sent are much more clear." She scrolls through the screen and brings up one of the shots I took on my phone the night West cracked open the Codex. "See this tiny white swish on the bottom right of the rune? It's not visible on the other images, so I didn't realize it right away. But once I confirmed it wasn't dust on your lens, I did some more digging and discovered that this little swish slightly alters the meaning. So in this case, the word 'kept' takes on a meaning more closely related to the word 'owned.'"

My gut clenches. "Owned? I don't understand."

I don't *want* to understand. My mind is already racing to form the conclusions, and then just as quickly railing against them.

"It's a dark fae rune of ownership often used by royal lines to mark their heirs," she says. "It's a property claim, so to speak."

"Like... like a fucking *brand*?" I grind out. *Fuck*. I close my eyes and sigh. "Forgive my language, Tatiana. This is just... it's very unsettling."

Her warm touch on my hand brings me back, and when I open my eyes, I find her watching me with a mix of compassion and concern.

"It *is* like a brand," she says softly, "but it wasn't branded onto the skin in the way you're thinking. It's the magic. In most royal fae, it never appears at all. But this person is obviously here, in our realm, and has been for some time. The longer they're separated from their homeland—from their bloodline and its connection to the land—the stronger the marking will become. The magic wants the bearer to be reunited with its people. Its home."

I bite back another curse. Draegan and Jude were right—it is like a tracking device.

"Even if its so-called people are monsters?"

"The magic makes no distinction." She sets the tablet on her desk and takes a seat behind it, steepling her hands over a pile of old journals. "Rook, this... rune bearer. They could be in danger."

I meet her gaze over the rim of my teacup and nod. "She," I finally say, realizing I'm going to have to reveal more about Westlyn than I'd hoped if I want Tatiana's help. "*She* could be in danger. And Tatiana? There's more." I recall the few details that Jude and Auggie were able to glean from Dr. Belinda Eckhardt. "Do you know anything about someone—or some *thing*—called the Moon Blessed? Possibly also known as the Peacebringer?"

Tatiana closes her eyes, her chin dropping to her chest. Now it's her turn to bite back the curse.

"Rook. Tell me this isn't connected to the rune. Tell me it's just a..." She shakes her head and sighs, her gaze slowly rising to meet mine across the dim space again. "What am I saying? Of course it's connected. There are no coincidences."

"No, I'm afraid not."

"It's an old demonic prophecy that goes back to the time when hell anointed its first princes. I don't know all the details, but it's got something to do with a belief that the royal lines of the demons and the dark fae actually share a common original ancestor, and that their lines were meant to one day reunite and reclaim what they believe is their right to rule over all realms."

"Demons and delusions of grandeur always go hand in hand, don't they?"

"That they do. Anyway, this 'Moon Blessed' was said to be the one who would ultimately bring about the reunion and lead the newly joined forces to glory—something like that. Let me see if I can find the exact verse. I've got some notes here somewhere—came across bits and pieces of it when I was preparing a joint lecture with the Vatican on the so-called legends of hell's royal lines."

She boots up her laptop and tabs through her files, finally finding what she's looking for. "Here we go. Most of it is gibberish, but here's the bit about the child, specifically."

A child conceived 'neath moon so bright
Born of the union of darkness and light
Blessed is the babe who inherits the crown
Blessed is the blood that brings the world down

With every line she reads, my heart sinks deeper. According to her mother, West was conceived under a bright fae moon. The union of darkness and light could easily represent her witch mother and dark fae father. She's got his noble blood, which isn't the same thing as royalty, but is pretty damn close—close enough that a single error in translation could make it possible that she's the one.

And if her rune is truly a royal claim...

No. I can't accept it. I won't. This conspiracy of dark fae and demons... No. That's not the life West deserves. It's not the life she wants.

"What about the Peacebringer?" I ask, desperate for a loophole. "Is there another prophecy?"

Tatiana shakes her head. "Peacebringer is just another name for the Moon Blessed. The child of the prophecy will bring peace—that's the idea."

"Demons and fae bringing peace? That makes no sense."

"Not peace for mankind, Rook. Their idea of peace is to completely obliterate humanity and anyone who stands in their way of the ultimate goal—the reclamation of what they believe is rightfully theirs. Theirs to rule. To claim."

"To own," I say, the image of West's rune burning behind my eyes.

Tatiana nods. "But... it's a prophecy, translated many times by many different people, lost and cobbled together again, re-translated... We don't know all the details." She thumbs through the pages of one of her journals, her eyes taking on a faraway glaze. "Prophecy, legend, myth, lies, history, facts, fables... Steeped in time like tea leaves. Eventually, it all begins to taste the same, doesn't it?"

"Do you think it's real? Regardless of the translations, do you believe this Moon Blessed is a real person destined to unite the demons and dark fae?"

She smiles kindly, her eyes twinkling. "As real as a gargoyle or an ancient vampire-witch."

Despite the warmth in her eyes, a chill seeps into my bones.

The legends may be wildly exaggerated or completely mistranslated or both, but there's always a kernel of truth buried in them.

And the fact remains... West *is* dark fae, and her birth coincides with the start of Hunter's treatments. Belinda Eckhardt all but named her. And everything in her mother's diaries points to her being the one.

It would explain Zorakkov's eagerness to claim her, particularly if the prophecy had something to do with joining the lines through marriage. The shadow mage society seemed desperate to see her wed Zorakkov as well, but as humans, they would be obliterated by the joining of the dark bloodlines. Wouldn't they?

And what does the Cerridwen Codex have to do with this? Why is Westlyn the only one able to read it?

Again, my mind is firing on all cylinders, trying to fill in the missing pieces and form the connections and just... protect the woman I love.

We finish our tea in silence, each lost in our own

thoughts. When my perimeter spell is ready, Tatiana bottles it up for me and walks me to the door, her hand curled around the crook of my arm.

"Smash this bottle anywhere on the property, and the spell will activate. It's good for two years, then you'll need to come see me again for a refresher."

"You did that on purpose," I tease. "You just wanted an excuse to get me over here again."

"A lady never tells, Rook."

Stepping onto the porch, I call up my human glamour and turn to her with a smile. "Thank you, as always, for your council. And for your friendship."

"And the tea and cookies," she says with a wink.

"Best part of the visit."

She laughs, but then her eyes turn serious. "Don't be a stranger. I'm good for more than just spells and old legends, and my discretion is above reproach."

I smile warmly. "Tatiana, the list of your virtues would fill my library many times over."

"I mean it, Rook," she says, and I know from the sudden ferocity in her tone she's dead serious. Pulling her shall tighter around her shoulders once more, she says, "Whatever lies ahead for you and your rune bearer, something tells me you're going to need allies in this. I just want you to remember you can *always* count me among them."

CHAPTER TWENTY-EIGHT

ROOK

By the time I finish up with Tatiana and get back to Blackmoor Manor, my wings are stiff and aching, my mind overloaded, and all I want to do is take West into my arms and kiss her until the sun rises.

After activating the perimeter spell, I head straight to the library in search of the woman who, according to the ancient vampire-witch, put the light back into my soulful brown eyes.

I give her another buzz to let her know I'm coming. She's at the door before I even set foot inside, her cheeks flush with color, her eyes dark with desire.

The moment I see her, I know Tatiana's news will have to wait.

Right now, nothing is more important than this. Than Westlyn. Than finally giving in to everything we've been feeling for weeks, everything I've so carefully danced around because I didn't know if she was truly ready for me.

"*Rook*," she breathes, and I can't tell whether that's relief or accusation in her voice. Then, in a whisper heavy with wanting, "You promised."

She's right. I've edged her all night long, teasing her senseless. Now, it's time to grant her a pleasure so intense, she'll still be feeling it long after I've turned to stone for the day.

Pretty sure I'll still be feeling it, too.

I wrap her in an embrace and lift her up, kicking the door closed behind me and turning off all the lights, leaving the library bathed in the glow of the crackling fire.

The scent of her desire, the feel of her smooth skin, the weight of her in my arms...

I don't know how the hell I've held out so long. I can't keep my hands off her another minute. I close my eyes and press my nose to her neck, breathing her in as I carry her to the library table, shove aside my books and papers, and lay her down.

Next to her, I place my phone. No, not because I'm expecting an urgent call—as if that could take me away from her tonight.

One glance at the device, and my girl knows *exactly* why it's there.

A soft sigh floats from between her lips as I slowly peel off her clothing, revealing her smooth, creamy skin. Her hair is loose tonight, black-and-silver waves fanning out behind her. The firelight dances in her eyes.

"You are so beautiful," I whisper, taking one more moment to drink her in, dark head to perfectly polished toes. "I've wanted you since the very first moment I saw you."

"Rook," she whispers again, bringing her hands up to cup her bare breasts. I turn the vibrator down to a slower pulse, and she arches her back, nearly writhing on the table. "Touch me. *Please* touch me. I can't handle you watching from the sidelines—not tonight."

"No, I've watched you long enough, Wild West. Dreamed of you, ached for you, night after night. I'm done watching." I lean over her on the table, brushing a lock of silver hair from her face.

And then, after imagining this moment for longer than I care to remember, I kiss her.

Her lips part on another sigh, and West reaches up and threads her fingers into my hair, pulling me closer. I deepen the kiss, exploring her soft, wet mouth, tasting her, memorizing her, every stroke of my tongue bringing us closer.

Behind us, the fire roars, the scent of flame and old parchment and all the things I love about my favorite place colliding with the scent of her, slowing twining around my heart and rooting me here.

It's everything.

It's perfect.

It's a kiss to remember, just like I promised her.

Finally pulling back for air, I whisper, "Do you trust me?"

Her eyes shine with emotion. She rises up and cups my face. "You know I do."

"Not just as a gargoyle sworn to protect you, West. I mean with your body. Your pleasure. All of it."

She smiles, and it feels like the sun on my skin. "All of it, Rook."

When I speak again, my voice is thick with lust, a growl I can barely contain. "Then lie back again for me, my wild girl. Spread your legs so I can see all the places *aching* for my tongue."

She does as I ask, revealing her pretty pussy and the full extent of her desire.

Fuck, she's so wet for me, her thighs are glistening.

With a soft chuckle, I say, "It seems I've left you in quite a state."

"You have *no* idea."

Skimming my claws down her thighs, I grip her knees and spread her even wider, then lower my mouth to her flesh, marking her inner thigh with a nip of my fangs.

"Rook," she gasps, arching against me.

I soothe the sting with a swirl of my tongue, then give her another bite. Another, another still, painting a trail of faint red marks along her inner thigh, then slowly moving to the other.

"You're... you're killing me," she breathes, wrapping her

hands around my horns and trying desperately to guide me *right* where she needs me most.

But I won't give in to her demands. Not yet.

"I plan to taste every inch of you tonight, West. And I'm going to take my sweet time making you come. Wringing out every drop of desire until you're utterly boneless."

I turn up the speed on the vibrator and blow a hot breath across her clit, making her gasp.

I've never wanted to taste anything so badly before. To bury my face between her thighs and find out exactly why Auggie and Jude are so damn addicted to her.

With another slow tease—agonizing for both of us—I trace a new path from her knee to her inner thigh with my tongue, then back down the other side, slowly turning up the speed on her vibrator.

"Goddess," she pants. "That feels so..." She trails off into a moan, fists tight around my horns, her scent washing over me in waves, and...

Fuck... I can't hold out. I need her in my mouth. Now.

With a tight grip on her thighs, I press my lips to her clit, sucking and kissing, slowly dragging my tongue down through her wet heat, her body jerking with every stroke as I lick and tease, but it's still not enough.

I want more.

With increasingly fevered thrusts, I fuck that hot pussy with my tongue, lapping her up, eating her, fucking *devouring* her as she rocks against my face, the sound of her heartbeat a frantic pulse as her blood races, her whole body spiraling toward the mind-blowing, soul-shattering release I've promised her all night...

"Rook!" she cries out. "I'm so close. I'm right there! I'm—"

"No." I force myself to stop, pulling back to meet her gaze as she bites back a groan of frustration. Her eyes are glassy, her cheeks pink, lips parted as she tries to catch her breath.

"It's torture, what you're doing to me," she whispers, her eyelids fluttering closed.

"Do you want me to stop?"

Her eyes fly open. "Don't you *dare* stop."

With another dark chuckle, I lower my mouth to her deliciously hot, wet center, and begin the game anew.

Savoring the taste of her, the silky feel of her in my mouth, I bring her to the brink more times than I can count, each one leaving her more breathless, more wound up, until I'm certain she can't take any more of my devilish teasing.

With one last long, satisfying lick, I finally release her thighs. I strip out of my loincloth and climb on top of her, the heat of her body radiating across my skin, and she parts her thighs for me once more, a sweet, seductive invitation I've denied myself for far too long.

"Okay?" I ask, tracing my thumb across her cheek.

She smiles up at me, her eyes alight with pleasure.

"Still trust me, then? Despite the torture?"

West laughs, her whole body alive with it. "For *now*, Professor Peepshow. Don't push your luck."

I kiss her again, soft and deep, then lower my mouth to her breasts, gently sucking one nipple, then the other. My hand drifts between her thighs, and I slide a finger inside her, slowly removing the vibrator. I drag it through her arousal, then tease it over her back entrance, gently working it inside the tight hole.

"Tell me how it feels," I whisper, giving the vibrator a bit more power.

"It feels... It's feels so fucking good, Rook. Like everything inside me is just... on fire." She moans beneath me, her heartbeat kicking up again. "I don't know how you made something so completely perfect."

"Because I've been watching you, West. How you move with Jude and Augustine. What makes you shudder and gasp when they touch you." I line the head of my aching cock up with her entrance. "I know *exactly* what your body wants. Exactly how to coax out every last bit of your pleasure."

She bites her lip and arches her hips and digs her nails into my forearms and I drive into her with the force of everything I've been holding back, everything I feel for her, every last hope and dream and fear and desire.

I'm not one to claim ownership, but the moment I'm inside her, I feel it.

Mine.

It's as though some deeply buried part of my soul

suddenly resurfaces and snaps into place, connecting me to her, overwhelming me with a sense of pure rightness.

The word echoes through me with every beat of my heart.

Mine. Mine. Mine.

I want my handprints on her ass, my bite on her shoulder, my cum dripping down her thighs, filling her soft pussy.

Mine.

The vibrator buzzes in her ass, radiating against my cock, urging me to fuck her harder, faster. I steal another kiss, swallowing her moans, her breath, the sound of my name on her lips. I kiss her neck, her shoulder, biting into her flesh. I grip her ass and drive in harder, only wanting more of her. All of her.

Everything.

She wraps her legs around my waist, angling to take me in deeper, arching her hips to meet my every thrust.

"Westlyn," I growl. "Fuck, you feel..." I let the words die, knowing they won't do any justice to what I'm feeling.

Forcing myself to slow my thrusts, I look into her eyes one more time, and my heart damn near bursts with the force of everything I feel for her.

For a brief instant, everything goes still and silent. West brushes her fingertips along my scruffy jaw, and a tear slides down her cheek.

"I love you, Rook Van Doren," she says. "More than all the pages in all the books in your library."

Fuck, it's everything, that declaration. Absolutely everything. And now, even if I had the words to do justice to my feelings, I wouldn't be able to form them. They'd only get tangled up inside.

She's still smiling at me, still touching my face.

Auggie may be the photographer, but I don't need a camera to remember this shot. I will never forget it.

The moment passes, and I move inside her again, everything in me wound tight, my muscles bunching, my cock throbbing, my balls heavy with the need to come.

I slide a hand between us, fingers slipping over her clit, the vibrator sending waves of pleasure through us both, her body pulsing around me, hot and slick as it clenches my cock, and once again, I push her right to the very precipice.

And this time, I let her fall.

"Come for me, wild girl," I growl, rubbing her clit faster. "Come for me and make me fucking *feel* how much you want this."

There's no hesitation. Starved for this release, her body obeys before her mind even processes the words.

"Rook!" she cries out, her heels digging hard into my lower back, her thighs trembling against my hips, her pussy clenching hard around my cock as the delayed orgasm finally explodes inside her, wave after pulsating wave, dragging me right over that white-hot edge with her.

One more deep thrust, and I come with a vicious snarl, unleashing a hot torrent that paints her insides and drips down her thighs, impossible to contain.

When her thighs finally stop trembling and my muscles

relax and the last waves of ecstasy finally begin to recede, I remove the vibrator and lay my cheek against her chest, my wings arcing over us as I count the beats of her heart and remind myself that she's real.

That she's here.

That she's ours.

CHAPTER TWENTY-NINE

ROOK

Slowly rising from the table, I grab a fire-warmed blanket from the back of the sofa and drape it over her. "Stay here," I say, pressing a soft kiss to her forehead. "I'll be right back."

After cleaning my new favorite toy, I run a hot bath in the library bathroom, then retrieve my wild witch from the table, leaving the blanket behind.

She sighs contentedly in my arms. "Boneless," she whispers, a faint smile touching the corners of her mouth.

"What do you mean?"

"You promised me boneless, and you delivered."

I laugh. "When does your professor ever disappoint?"

Another contented sigh. "He doesn't."

Gently, I set her in the tub, watching her limbs unfurl in the water.

"Lean back," I say, kneeling beside the tub. "I've got you."

She does as I ask, and I wash her hair, massaging her scalp and neck, then slowly guiding her head under the faucet to rinse.

"What time is it?" she asks with an adorable yawn.

"There's no hurry. We've got about an hour before sunrise yet."

"An hour?" She sits up, turning to face me. "That's no time at all! I was hoping you'd have time to tell me about your meeting with Tatiana."

A chill presses against my heart as I recall everything Tatiana shared tonight. The rune. The prophecy.

But there's too much to say, too much to unpack, and I'm not about to try with less than an hour.

Tomorrow. It can wait until tomorrow.

"Rook?" she presses.

Swallowing down my worries, I cup her face and say, "I mean, we *could* spend our last hour together talking about fae and demon lore, but honestly?" I lean in and brush a soft kiss to her mouth, my heartbeat stuttering. "I'd much rather spend it telling you how I fell for you."

West's eyes shimmer in the moonlight, an unspoken question behind them.

"Yes, Wild West. I fell for you, too. I've *determined* it with *certainty*."

Her answering smile spreads from ear to ear. She knows I never use those particular words lightly.

"The moment you walked into the library that first time," I say softly, stroking her cheek, "your entire face lit up at the sight of all those books. I knew right then we were kindred spirits."

She nods, a laugh escaping.

"Your mind was the first thing to fully captivate me." I trace my thumb across her forehead, then down to her jaw. "Your inquisitiveness, your sharp wit, the way your brow furrows when you ask questions or lose yourself in one of the old tomes."

I kiss the space between her eyes, then slide my fingers into her wet hair.

"Your eyes entranced me next—like the tranquil seas of the world's most beautiful islands. And your kiss?" I draw her close, pressing my lips to the corner of her mouth. "Even for someone who's spent fifteen centuries with his nose in books, I don't think I've ever come across the right words to describe what it feels like to kiss you."

Her eyes glaze with emotion.

"Do you remember what I said to you the other night, after I watched you with Auggie and Jude, and you wanted me to kiss you?" I ask.

"You... you said you've been waiting for someone like me your whole immortal life."

"No. Not someone *like* you, Westlyn Avery. You. I've been waiting for *you*. This perfect, beautiful, inquisitive, demanding, sassy witch. We've *all* been waiting for you. Nothing ever felt right until you showed up, and now you're ours. Do you have any idea what you mean to us? To me?" I shake my head, still shocked at the wonder of how she came to us, at the force of my feelings for her. "For so long, I felt like I've been wandering an empty, barren wasteland. I didn't even realize I was lost until I met you. Falling for you felt like coming home. And now that I'm here, I never want to be lost again. You are my home. My heart. There's nothing I won't do for you. *Nothing*. Because I didn't just fall for you, Wild West. I love you. I *love* you. More than all the pages in all the books in all the libraries in the realms."

With that, she pulls me into the tub with her, wraps her arms around my neck, and kisses me until I'm boneless, too, and the first signs of sunrise glitter on the distant horizon, and I finally tear myself away from her and head up to the roof, knowing with a deep and heavy dread that when the moon rises on a brand new night, I'm going to have to break her heart.

CHAPTER THIRTY

AUGUSTINE

Moon Blessed. The Peacebringer. Righting the ancient wrongs. Death to all who refuse to kneel before the two great lords...

Belinda Eckhardt's ominous rants take on a whole new meaning in light of Rook's recent discoveries.

Draegan and Jude have been in the city since last night trailing various shadow magic society members in hopes of finding more intel on the archmage and Detective Reedsy. So, over a meal of butternut squash soup and roasted vegetables, Rook told me and West about his occult studies friend, Tatiana—the vampire-witch who's apparently known about our existence for a century—and everything she shared with him last night about the so-called Moon Blessed prophecy.

About West's rune.

Kept. Owned. A property claim.

Those were Tatiana's exact words.

I wanted to find the nearest working fae portal and jump right the fuck through it, hunt down every last Wintermoon prick, and rip their fucking dark hearts out of their chests. But that would only get me killed and put West even more on the radar.

West took it all in stride, like she always does. Asking questions. Taking notes. Trying to make connections. She's like Rook in that way, I realize. Her mind on a constant quest for truth and knowledge.

But I know it weighs on her. Not knowing who she is, what fate has in store for her. After dinner, she told us she needed some air, and went out to walk the grounds with Lucinda and Huxley, hoping to clear her head.

Now, two hours later, I find her in the apple orchard, quietly pacing among the stately trees as her ravens investigate the fallen apples with great interest.

She turns toward me as she hears my approach, her face bathed in moonlight, hair shimmering around her shoulders, and for a moment I just watch her, memorizing the way the light dances in her eyes, the gentle flutter of her hair stirred by a soft breeze.

"Hey," she says softly, reaching up for a hug. "I'm glad you're here."

I gather her in my arms, pressing a kiss to the top of her head. "Just checking on you. If you need more time alone, I can—"

"No. Stay. I was about to head back, anyway."

"Feeling better?"

"All things considered? Yes." She takes my hand, and we walk beneath the boughs, leaving the ravens to their apple treasures. "I should probably be more freaked out—and don't get me wrong—I *am* freaked out. But knowledge is power, right? I might not like what the knowledge has to say, but it's better than being kept in the dark and making up stories, playing the 'what if' game."

"We don't know for sure though," I say. "This prophecy... there's a lot that could be misinterpreted. And we don't know what the whole thing says."

"No. But again, it's a start, and it's a lot more than we knew yesterday, and a *hell* of a lot more than we knew on my wedding night. So I'm counting it as a win. Besides, it sounds like Rook's friend Tatiana might be able to find out more. Rook was going to check in with her again and see what else she can dig up on the prophecy and the royal demon lines."

We stop under a particularly large tree, and West gazes up into the branches, heavy with ripe fruit. Soon, they'll fall, and the frost will come, and then the snows, encasing my beloved trees in ice.

I hope we're all still here to see it.

"The demon and fae thing," she says. "It sounds crazy, but I get it. Together, they'd be a pretty unstoppable force. But the shadow mage thing is still a mystery. And Eloise? Total wildcard. Other than social status, I can't figure out her motives at all." She laughs, but it's as cold as the autumn breeze. "Then again, social status can be a powerful motivator. Take it from someone who never had any."

"You might not have had status, but you also didn't resort to scheming against innocents, paying to have a young girl bullied into submission, or aligning with dark organizations."

"I can't say for sure that I wouldn't have, though. Right? If the opportunity fell into my lap?"

"No. No way. You're too good a person for that. You—"

"We can tell ourselves how good we are all day long, Augs. But all that really means is we've made certain choices up to this point. Anything could change that. Anything." She meets my gaze again and shrugs. "I guess that's why I'm still struggling with the idea of cutting all ties with Brian. I'm still looking for the good in him, especially now that I know what my mother did to him. Some part of me still wants to believe he actually cared about me, just like she said. Is that completely stupid?"

"To want love and respect from the man who raised you as your father? No. It's not stupid to want it. But chasing after it and basing your sense of self-worth around its lack can be a dangerous path."

"I just... I still don't want to accept that he sold me out. That he betrayed me, even though I wouldn't blame him at this point. My mother betrayed *him*. I'm a living, breathing representation of that. It probably still hurts him to this day. Don't you think?"

She's looking up at me with those big, turquoise eyes

like she wants me to say something comforting. Some platitude about time healing all wounds and forgiveness being a balm for the heart.

But I can't lie to her.

Yeah, sometimes, old wounds *do* fade. Old betrayals are forgiven or forgotten, or both.

But most of the time, the pain is always lingering just beneath the surface, waiting for you to let your guard down. To hear a few bars of an old song or smell an ingredient from a dish you haven't cooked in a century, and suddenly you're reliving the worst moments of your life in all their blade-sharp glory after you'd been insisting for decades you'd made your peace.

Grief and betrayal, loss and death... They grip us. They mark us. They whisper their stories in our hearts for eternity.

And they never let us truly forget.

"I think," I say instead, scooping her up and holding her tight, "I'd much rather kiss you than talk about betrayals and pain."

A smile breaks across her face, and she leans in close, teasing me with a feather-light kiss before pulling away.

"Oh, I don't think so, witchling." I set her on her feet and back her up against the tree, caging her in with my arms, then claiming her mouth in a bruising kiss. She parts her lips for me, moaning into my mouth, her fingers twining through my hair.

"Hungry," she pants, breaking our kiss. "You make me so… hungry."

A soft chuckle rumbles through me. "You know I'm happy to cook you anything you'd—"

"Not for food, Augs." She reaches for the zipper on her sweatshirt, giving me a look that leaves no room for misinterpretation.

Her sweatshirt falls away, leaving her topless in the moonlight, her bare skin glowing. Not with magic. Not with runes. Just her. Just my witchling.

I lean in close again, dragging my nose up the slope of her neck, kissing a path to her ear.

"I swear I didn't come out here for this, witchling," I whisper. "But you *are* half naked, and I *am* hard, and, well…" I kiss her again, skimming my hands up her ribs, brushing my knuckles across her nipples. She arches into my touch with a gasp, and I drop to my knees before her, my mouth closing around one of her dark peaks.

"That's… perfect," she breathes. "Goddess, you feel so good, Auggie."

"All part of my master plan to keep you begging for more." I kiss my way to her other breast, grazing her nipple with my fangs before sucking it between my lips.

"It's working," she says. "*Please* give it to me. More. All of it."

The scent of her desire mingles with the scent of the apples, of the night sky, of the damp leaves and the cold earth and everything I love about this place, my home, my heart. Overwhelmed with a feeling I can't even describe, I sweep her off her feet and lay her down in the leaves, descending on her once more in a flurry of hot, ravenous kisses before flipping us so she's straddling me, grinding against my cock, her sweet little moans driving me fucking wild, and—

The snap of a twig and movement behind another apple tree snags my attention, the barest hint of a wing outlined in the shadows.

"I think we've got a visitor, witchling," I whisper, nodding toward the tree.

"In that case, better put on a good show. I'd hate to disappoint him."

"Rook *is* a tough critic—so I've heard."

"The toughest." She laughs. "But now that he's here..." She turns toward the tree, where the unmistakable form of a gargoyle has finally begun to emerge.

Flashing him a devilish grin, she says, "Come out of the shadows and play with us, Rook. We're just getting started."

But when the gargoyle finally steps into the moonlight and reveals himself, it's not Rook watching us at all.

It's Draegan.

And something tells me he *definitely* doesn't want to play.

"Draegan!" Westlyn leaps off me and covers her breasts —instinct more than embarrassment, I suspect. "We were just talking about our research, and... um..."

"Oh, for fuck's *sake*." Anger flares in his eyes, his body rigid with it, but he's not angry at us.

No. He's angry at the fact that he's irrevocably turned on and madly in love with her, and too fucking pig-headed to do anything about *either* situation.

"Did you need something, Drae?" I ask, not bothering to hide my irritation. "Because as you can see, we're kind of busy with our... research. So if you don't mind..."

"Oh, really?" He lets out a bitter laugh. "Well! Pardon the inconvenient interruption of your so-called *research*, but believe it or not, some of us actually have *important* things to discuss with Miss Avery. Important, mission-critical things that don't require either party stripping bare beneath a nearly full moon in my apple orchard and rutting each other like a pair of—"

A loud squawk cuts him off, followed by another, and I just about lose my shit at the sight of two ravens chasing a grown-ass gargoyle through the orchard, all the way back to Blackmoor.

"Guess we know whose side *they're* on," I say, still laughing when Draegan finally disappears out of sight, undoubtedly locking himself inside.

But when I turn back to West, it's clear she's not seeing the humor in this.

In fact, she looks like she wants to tear off Drae's wings, roast them in the fire, and feed them to him.

I run a hand over her head and sigh. "I'll go talk to him."

"No." She gets to her feet and tugs the sweatshirt back

on, covering her beautiful breasts—yet *another* thing I'm adding to the lists of reasons why I'm going to beat Draegan's ass. Then, with a determined gleam in her eyes, she pushes up her sleeves and says, "*I'm* going. I've got a few choice words for *Daddy* Drae."

CHAPTER THIRTY-ONE

DRAEGAN

My bathroom door bangs open with the force of a hurricane, slamming against the wall and rattling the glass shower door.

I've got my tail wrapped around my cock, my hands braced against the glass, my muscles tight with the need for release...

And now I've got the little mortal standing in the middle my bathroom, hands on her hips, cheeks red with exertion, leaves stuck in her tousled hair, those mesmerizing eyes glaring at me as though she can't *wait* to read me the riot act.

The scent of her only winds me tighter—apples and damp earth and rage and the unmistakable tang of lust.

Of all the times to storm the castle, little mortal...

"Bloody *hell*, woman," I growl. "That door was closed for a reason."

Her gaze roams down the glass, her eyes widening as she undoubtedly realizes what I've been up to.

She recovers quickly, schooling her features into a mask of annoyance.

"Oh, you don't like when someone barges in on you during a private moment and gets all rude about it?" She hops up on the vanity counter, folds her arms over her chest, and continues to glare at me through the glass. Then, with a mocking sneer, "Well! Pardon the inconvenient interruption of your mission-critical shower! Carry on!"

Carry on. Right.

"What the hell do you want?" I demand.

"I'm not the one who stormed into the orchard acting like the house was on fire, flinging insults when we didn't immediately drop everything and bow to your every whim. So why don't you tell *me* what *you* want before I take the scissors to your five-thousand-thread-count sheets?"

Damn it. She's not going to let me off the hook. Not going to give me a fucking inch.

I turn off the water and release my aching cock from the tail's firm grip, for all the good it does me. Having her this close to me when I'm naked and wet and she's pissed off and glaring at me like she's about to set my cock on fire?

Fuck, my balls are throbbing for her.

"I wanted to give you an update on Detective Reedsy," I say, turning slightly to keep my rock-hard cock from pressing up against the glass.

"Well? Don't keep me in suspense."

"We received word from our contact in customs that he's hiding out in Argentina. He bought a round-trip ticket, though—if he sticks to the itinerary, he'll be back in a week. Jude suspects he's looking for property down there, probably to relocate permanently."

"What happens when he comes back?"

"We'll be waiting for him."

She sighs, some of her anger dissipating as she hops off the counter. Heading for the exit without so much as another glance in my direction, she says, "Thanks for the update. Next time, try to be less... less *you* about it."

Fuck. She's leaving again. Turning her back and walking away from me like she always does.

Because you keep pushing *her away, you daft bastard...*

No. Not tonight. Not now.

"Not so fast, little mortal." Ignoring the state of my cock, I step out of the shower, water sluicing down my skin and puddling on the tile floor. "I told you what I wanted. Now it's your turn."

"I don't want anything from you," she says, refusing to turn around to face me.

I take a step closer, then another, so close my breath stirs the back of her hair. A rogue leaf lingers, and I resist the urge to pull it free. "You wouldn't have left Augustine and his hard-on to fend for themselves in the orchard if that were true." Then, teeth gritted against the scent of her skin, the desire she's stirring painfully to life inside me, "So dispense with the attitude and tell me what it is you want from me, Miss Avery."

Tell me you still want me. Tell me you forgive me for being a world-class arsehole, again and again and again. Tell me you're still thinking about the last time we touched...

"Are you asking me for the truth?" She finally turns to face me head-on, her eyes lasering in on mine, then slowly raking over my form. "Or some inane pleasantries that will make you feel better about yourself?"

"From you, I want the truth. Always."

"I want the truth from you too, Draegan." She meets my gaze again and sighs. "That's it. Honesty, pure and simple. Not just about what's going on with Reedsy and the Forsythes, but about what's going on in here." She presses her palm to my heart, her touch as soothing as ever. "I want you to stop acting like a jealous dickhead whenever you see me with the other guys, because you know damn well I'm yours, too. I want you to stop avoiding me just because feelings are uncomfortable sometimes. I want you to look me in the eyes and tell me—"

"Tell you *what*?" I grip her wrist, sliding my thumb along the delicate skin, unleashing an involuntary shiver that rolls through her body from head to toe. "That I can't stop thinking of you?" I whisper. "That the remembered sound of you *begging* me to touch you is a lullaby that soothes my darkest nightmares?" I step closer, lifting her up and setting her back on the vanity counter, dragging my nose down along the slope of her neck. "That the scent of your skin haunts me so violently, I find myself inventing excuses just to be near you—another update on our enemies' whereabouts, some inane question, an argument always at the ready if only to keep you in my presence, to see that fire light up your eyes?"

She swallows hard, and I brush my lips over her throat, her pulse thrumming just beneath the surface.

"To tell you," I whisper, "that the very feel of your name on my lips makes my heart beat so fast, I fear it might burst before I get a chance to touch you again?"

She opens her mouth to speak, but I brush my thumb across her lips, silencing her.

"You asked me to kiss you the other night, and I refused. Twice. Not a moment passes when I don't regret it. And *that*, Miss Avery, is the honest truth."

Hurt flickers in her eyes, and I curse myself for bringing it up again. For reminding her what a bastard I've been to her.

But then the hurt vanishes, blinked away so fast I can't even be sure it was ever there at all.

A cold grin slides across her lips, almost cruel. It's so unlike her I stumble backward.

"And you think I'm going to let you kiss me now?" she taunts. "After the way you've been acting? Is that what's happening here?"

"I think..." I move in close again, quickly reclaiming the ground I lost, refusing to back down. "You're still craving that kiss just as much as I am."

"Ha! Whatever pretty lies you need to tell yourself to get through the night."

"It's not a pretty lie, Miss Avery. I *am* craving it. I haven't *stopped* craving it. And neither have you."

"If it's really a kiss you're after..." She folds her arms and puts a bare foot to my chest, shoving me backward. Then, in a voice as cold as her smile, "*Beg* me for it."

The fire in her eyes is back, and I know we're both thinking of that night in my office. Of all the hot, filthy things I did to her on my desk...

Fucking hell.

Maybe I don't know how to be honest about what I'm feeling.

Maybe she doesn't know how to stay away from a man who can't stop hurting her.

But *this* game? We've always been good at this game.

So fucking good.

So for now, I cling to it. Relish it. Own it as readily as I'm about to own *her*.

"Mmm," I murmur. "You want to put Daddy in his place, then? Teach me a lesson?"

A careless shrug. A disinterested glance at her fingernails. "You're the one who's so desperate for my kiss, *Daddy*. The question is... how far are you willing to go to get it?"

"If you think I won't get on my knees for you, Westlyn Avery..." I grab her heel and lift it to my shoulder, then slide in close to her once more, nestling my cock snugly between her thighs.

"What... what are you doing?" she breathes, all of her feigned disinterest evaporating like steam on the glass shower door.

"Showing you just how far I'm willing to go to get that kiss." Then, grabbing her other leg and hitching it over my shoulder, I drop to the floor before her. "If you want to end this, all you've got to do is use your words."

"Fuck off."

"Now, now," I say. "We both know those are *not* the words to make me stop. Try again."

She slides a hand through my hair, then fists it tightly, glaring down at me with a mix of lust and fury, the two emotions at such odds in her eyes I'm honestly not sure which one will win out.

"I swear to the goddess... I *hate* you sometimes."

A dark chuckle rumbles through my chest. "Hate me all you want. It doesn't change the fact that you *love* the way I make you feel."

I'm on her like a madman, sharp claws shredding her thin shorts and panties, baring her to me.

She gasps and spreads her thighs, and I descend, lips and tongue and fangs and hot, frantic breaths, licking and sucking, nibbling her silky skin.

With tight fists, she strokes my horns and rocks against my face, my name falling from her lips again and again in harsh, desperate whispers, as if she doesn't know whether to push me away or beg me for more.

Well. Now that I've gotten such a fine taste, I'm not about to let her push me away.

I lash her with my tongue, spearing her, fucking her, taking, taking, *taking* until she's all I can taste. All I can feel. All I've ever fucking known.

She shatters around my tongue with no more than a last, desperate gasp, her thighs spasming around my head, fingernails digging into my scalp as she comes for me, and I growl against her hot flesh and greedily lick up every last drop of her arousal.

Mine.

As soon as the breath returns to her lungs, she pushes me away and hops off the vanity counter, the lust in her eyes clearing as quickly as a storm chased off by the sun.

"That was the *last* time you ever touch me like that, Draegan."

My hackles rise and I get to my feet, towering over her. "Don't you dare speak to me as if you weren't *every* bit as eager for it as I was."

"I'm not denying I wanted you. *Goddess*, I wanted you. I *always* want you. I'm simply reminding myself—reminding *both* of us—what a terrible idea it is to—"

"To *what*?" I whisper darkly, crowding her back against the wall, my wings closing in around her like a cage. "To kiss? To touch?" Then, wrapping my hand around her throat and bringing my mouth to her ear, "To writhe and moan and *fuck* until we're both filthy and trembling and breathless? Because that's what you're thinking about now, is it not? What it felt like when I had you bent over my desk, filling you up with so much cum you didn't think you'd ever take another step without feeling the hot slide of it running down your thighs?"

Her pulse responds to the press of my thumb, a frantic drumbeat that unleashes another growl deep in my chest. "*Fuck.* Do you have any idea what you *do* to me, little mortal?"

"I... I don't... I'm..." Her eyelids flutter closed, her breath hot on my skin.

I spin her around and pin her face-first against the wall, grinding against her lithe body, burying my face in her hair, inhaling the scents of the apple orchard and her raw, pulsating desire.

"Lie to me with your words if that's what you need to do," I continue softly, dragging my hand down her chest, her belly, dipping between her thighs and stroking until her arousal coats my fingers. "But your body speaks only the truth."

"Draegan," she moans.

"Tell me to stop," I command. "Use your words."

Another shuddering breath. A shake of her head.

Still fucking her with one hand, I skim the other one up her throat and shove three fingers into her mouth. She closes her lips around them, her tongue gliding over my skin like hot velvet as she sucks me, harder and faster, deeper, and... oh, *fuck*... she's unraveling me again, as she *always* manages to unravel me...

"Tell me you don't want this," I grind out, pushing my cock between her thighs, teasing her entrance. "Tell me you don't want this and I'll release you."

I slide my fingers out of her mouth and hold my breath, waiting for a fucking eternity for the answer that will either set me free or send me to my fucking grave.

And then, finally...

"Fuck off," she whispers, arching her backside to give me full access.

One deep, hard thrust, and I'm buried to the fucking hilt.

She curses again, whispers my name like she's casting a spell to send me straight to hell, and I capture her wrists in one hand and pin them above her head, my other hand still working her clit as I fuck her against the wall.

I'm not soft and slow. I'm not appreciating the softness of the fine hairs on the back of her neck or marveling at the cruel beauty of her scars or tracing delicate patterns over the curves of her shoulder. I'm absolutely *savage*, claiming her with every hot, punishing thrust, slamming her against the wall as I take her faster, stroking her clit with a fevered touch, chasing her like a predator to the very top of that cliff...

Her body clenches around me as the orgasm rocks her to the core, and I bite down on her shoulder and I fucking *explode*, cursing the night I ever laid eyes on this beautiful, impossible, infuriating woman.

A moment passes in silence.

Then another.

Slowly, I drag myself out and take a step back, trying to chase down my thoughts. Trying to find something to say that won't send her bolting out of here again.

But when she turns around to face me, I know from the fire in her eyes that those words just don't exist.

"You can't go around saying and doing whatever the hell you want," she snaps, "hurting everyone in your path, then just sweeping in with your dirty words and dirty mouth and tidying it all up with sex."

Her cheeks are stained a dark plum, her hair a wild tangle, and I can't help but smile, even though I know it's only going to get me into more hot water.

"*Amazing* sex," I point out. "Utterly mind-blowing, if you must know."

"Oh!" She laughs, bitter and harsh. "Someone thinks rather highly of himself."

"Are you denying it?"

"Doesn't matter."

"Are you certain? Are you—"

"Hot waffles!" she snaps. "Yeah, that's right. Hot waffles. I said it, okay? I'm using my words because you need to *stop*.

I can't take another minute of you running me in circles until my head spins. Game over, I'm tapping out, I'm done."

Fuck. She's right. Of course she's right, and once again, I've managed to hurt her. To reel her in close... and push her right back out again.

"Westlyn, wait. I... I don't mean to play games."

"Oh, really? Does that mean you're ready to be fully honest with me now?"

"I've never lied to you."

"Not lying is not the same thing as actually *admitting* the truth."

"The truth about what?"

"Use your words, Draegan," she taunts.

I say nothing.

She huffs out a breath and shakes her head, her eyes glazing. Sadness? Anger? Regret? It's all so mixed up now I can't tell the difference.

She turns to leave, but I grab her wrist.

"Let. Me. Go," she grinds out, the hatred in her voice too much to bear, even for me.

I do as she asks and take a step backward, giving her space. Waiting her out. Waiting for her to turn back around, look up at me with those big, blue-green eyes, and crash right back into my arms.

But in the span of a few precious heartbeats, the little brat is stalking out of my bathroom, out of my suite, and slamming the door behind her so hard it makes my teeth rattle.

And here I remain, the honest words she so desperately needs to hear lodged uselessly in my throat.

I can't stop touching you.

I can't stop wanting you.

I can't stop finding ways to be near you because I'm bloody well in love with you, Westlyn Avery, and that *shall be my undoing.*

CHAPTER THIRTY-TWO

WESTLYN

The *incident* with Draegan—yes, I'm calling it an incident; there's no other word for what that infuriating man does—leaves me keyed up and wrung out in more ways than one.

I spend the next hour pacing in my room, indigo magic crackling in my palms. It's darker tonight, restless, as if it can sense my mood.

It's hungry, too. Eager to break something.

Not break, my moon. Devour...

I startle at the words as they slice through my mind, not recognizing them as my own conscious thoughts.

My moon?

Great. It's bad enough the cold, cruel fae haunts my nightmares. Now I've got his evil voice whispering to me during waking hours, too?

Grabbing my amulet, I close my eyes and shake out my

hands, desperate to shed this excess energy, this weird magic. The amulet warms against my skin, and when I open my eyes again, I find the darker magic dissipating, finally settling in to a faint glow at my fingertips.

Sleep. I just need to sleep. Start fresh tomorrow. Draegan and Jude don't even know about what Rook learned from Tatiana yet, and I have no idea if he'll have a chance to speak with them tonight.

Tomorrow, we're all going to have to come together and make a real plan. Not just for finishing the Codex transcription and figuring out what it all means, but for getting our hands on the rest of this so-called prophecy. Demons and fae teaming up against the world? That's not going to end well for anyone. We need to get ahead of it, if we can.

Whether I'm the so-called "chosen one" or not.

After a quick shower to calm my still-raw nerves, I pull on a pair of yoga pants and one of Jude's T-shirts and crawl between the sheets, grateful to have a night alone in my own room.

A night where I can just... reset.

But sleep takes forever to find me, and when that elusive mistress finally claims me, she drags me into depths so dark and murky, I'm certain I'll never again see the light.

I dream of the city in ruins again, of people marching through the streets while dark fire burns down the world around them.

I dream of children screaming for their parents,

watching in sheer terror as fae armies gut them with swords.

I dream of my gargoyles turning to stone and crumbling to dust before my eyes.

I dream of Zorakkov, chaining me to him for eternity, beating me, torturing me, carving my flesh to summon his minions from the bowels of hell.

And I dream of Judgment. The Tarot card with the naked woman rising from a cauldron of flames, a phoenix from the ashes.

Only it's no longer just a Tarot card—it's as real as anything I've ever experienced. I'm standing with her in the center of her cauldron—a massive iron structure as large as a house, the top open to reveal a starless sky and a full, blood-red moon.

"Blood on the moon," she says, reaching for my hand. Flames ripple along her skin, but her touch doesn't burn me. She's kind. Calming.

"What does it mean?" I ask.

"You have a task to accomplish. You mustn't fail."

"I won't," I insist, resolute, though I have no idea what I'm promising. "But what—"

"Shh." She presses a flame-touched finger to my lips. "We are not alone."

The walls of her cauldron flicker, my bedroom coming into view.

I'm on the knife's edge between asleep and awake, my

mind spinning. I try to get back to the woman, to my task, but something is keeping me here, tugging at my consciousness...

The floor creaks as someone kneels beside the bed. A strong hand smoothes my hair, warm breath tickling my lips.

The scent of him envelopes me.

Draegan.

With a soft sigh, I reach for the gargoyle before me, wrapping my hands around his horns and urging him closer.

"Draegan," I whisper, slowly blinking up at him. The room is pitch black; I can just barely make out his silhouette. He doesn't utter a word, and for a moment I think my eyes are playing tricks on me, but no. It's definitely him. His presence is overwhelming.

"Sleep, little mortal," he whispers, stroking my hair. "Just sleep."

I open my mouth to tell him no, to ask him to stay, to promise him whatever terrible things we've said and done to each other don't matter. But I'm tired. So very, very tired, and the woman in the cauldron is beckoning me back to that dark, quiet place inside me, and I slip back under her thrall before I can speak another word.

I'm back in the cauldron now, but it's no longer dark and quiet.

Fire rages around us, and she lifts her palms to the sky, urging the flames higher.

"It is time," she says, and I nod.

"I'm ready."

The world spins around me, and when I feel my feet on solid ground again, I open my eyes to find myself in the library.

It's dark, save for the violet light surrounding the Codex.

It calls to me from its position on the table, and I move without thinking, pressing my palms to either side of it. The words on the page glow bright, dancing before my eyes.

The woman from the cauldron is at my side again, but when I glance up at her, she transforms into the dark fae that's been haunting my nightmares for weeks. Tall. Reed-thin, framed with lean muscles. Black hair falls past his shoulders. His mouth is a cruel red slash.

Tonight, I'm not afraid of him, though.

Tonight, he feels... familiar.

Everything is unfolding as it should be...

"Sometimes," he says in that same otherworldly voice, "in order to build what *could* be, we must first destroy what *is*."

The words call the rune on the back of my neck to life, sizzling my skin and unlocking something deep inside me. Something ancient. Something right. My palms begin to glow bright against the book, the same dark indigo magic from before, only this time I'm not restless.

I welcome it. Call it forth. Nurture it.

Beneath my touch, the letters dancing on the pages of the Codex settle into a verse.

A child conceived 'neath moon so bright
Born of the union of darkness and light
Blessed is the babe who inherits the crown
Blessed is the blood that brings the world down

I recognize the words from Tatiana's notes about the prophecy, but then another verse appears beneath the first, and I read it aloud like a chant.

Like a spell.

For that, I realize, is what it is.

And *this*, I realize, is my great task.

I will not fail.

Blood of my blood, my magic, my fire
I call unto you, my king and my sire
Return to this realm to claim what is ours
By flame and by force, so shall we devour

I repeat it three times, the magic in my hands growing stronger and stronger until the soft glow turns into indigo flames. They lick up my arms and across my chest, filling me with strength. With power.

The fae beside me smiles, his silver eyes glittering like precious jewels.

"What must I do?" I whisper. I don't recognize my own

voice.

Am I still dreaming? Is this a vision? A nightmare?

Something stirs in the farthest recesses of my mind.

This is wrong. Wrong. Wrong...

No. I shake my head, dismissing the irritating thoughts. Nothing has ever been more right.

The flames in my hands surge, reflecting in the fae's black eyes, his cruel smile stretching into a malicious grin I can't help but mirror.

"Burn it, my moon," he commands. "Burn it all."

Without a thought, I turn to the nearest bookshelf and press my palms against it.

The old tomes ignite immediately.

I move to another shelf and set it ablaze, watching as my dark flames chew through book after book, turning every story, every poem, every passage into ash. Soon, the entire library is engulfed, the smell of burning parchment and wood filling my senses, magic tingling across my skin.

A terrifying, otherworldly laugh bubbles up from inside me as smoke fills my lungs. Heat surges over my face, and I drop to my knees and raise my palms to the sky, ready to burn and rise from the ashes.

Tap tap tap tap tap.

Tap tap tap.

The sound is like a jackhammer against my skull. Fire licks my face, heat coating my neck and chest with sweat.

Heat. Fire. No...

"No. No!" I open my eyes, wincing against the assault of bright sunlight. Images of Rook's library flicker through my mind... Books burning... Wooden beams crashing to the ground...

And then they fade away.

I suck in a shuddering breath. It wasn't real. None of it was real.

Goddess. Just another nightmare. A terrible fucking nightmare.

Relief crashes through me, but... wait.

Sunlight? Why is their sunlight on my face?

I sleep during the day, and even if I didn't, my windows aren't positioned to let in the morning sunlight...

I'm not in my bed. I can't move. Why can't I fucking move?

I glance down at my aching body, my eyes still trying to adjust to the bright light. I'm bound to a heavy wooden chair, ropes around my wrists and ankles, chains around my middle.

Panic skitters across my chest.

I take another deep breath. The scent of fire clings to my hair. My mouth is parched, lips coated with ash.

No. This can't be happening.

Tap tap. Tap tap tap.

That sound again... It's coming from a window high overhead. I crane my neck to find the source of it—that must've been what woke me up. Squinting against the too-bright light, I finally make out my raven.

It's Jean-Pierre. He's alone.

The panic kicks up a notch. Where are Lucinda and Huxley? Where the fuck am I? Where are the guys? What happened last night?

I cast around the space, desperate to orient myself.

Think, girl. Think.

High, wood-beamed ceilings. Ornate candlelit chandeliers. A nave full of wooden pews.

And the altar my chair has been set upon.

I know this place...

Realization crashes through me, and I gasp.

I'm in Thornwood Cathedral. The sight of my failed wedding. The very place where my family tried to bind me to—

"Good morning, little one," comes the cold hiss, and a tall, lean figure steps out of the sacristy.

It's not Zorakkov, though. Not Eloise or the Archmage.

It's *him*.

Dressed in luxurious black silks with deep violet adornments, his gait smooth and commanding, the dark fae from my nightmares joins me on the altar.

Cold, silver eyes peer down at me, his gaze as sharp as the sword strapped to his hip. Long black hair frames his handsome face, setting off his shimmering skin.

A golden crown rests atop his head, studded with blood-red jewels.

Everything inside me revolts, and I shrink beneath his cutting glare, beneath the sudden realization that damn near grips me by the throat.

He's not just the fae from my nightmares. The fae I saw in Eloise's visions.

He's the dark fae king. Verrick of Wintermoon.

"You're not real," I whisper, struggling against my bonds. The chains rattle, the rope cutting into my wrists. "You're just... just a nightmare."

"I am many things," he says, his ancient voice like cold steel against my spine, making me stop struggling and sit up straight again. "But 'just a nightmare' is not one of them, I'm afraid. I'm as real as the ancient ground beneath this cathedral."

"But you... you can't travel to this realm. The portals... I thought..."

"I don't need the portals, child. Only you."

"Me? But... how?"

He grins, and the rune at the back of my neck flares to painful attention. "You called me here with your spell."

"No. I wouldn't have done that. Even if I wanted to, I wouldn't know the first thing about..." My words falter as the rest of the nightmare crashes through my memory.

No, not a nightmare.

Real. It was all real.

The Codex. The indigo magic. The spell. The fire. The library.

Oh, Goddess. The library...

My heart shatters, tears spilling down my cheeks.

"I've heard a great deal about you," he says, looking at me like I'm some rare specimen under the microscope. "Yet it pales in comparison to the real thing."

"Likewise," I hiss.

My reply seems to please him. "Ah. You know who I am, then?"

"I know *exactly* who you are," I say with a sneer I can't be bothered to hide. This is the foul beast who cursed the men I love. Who destroyed their lands and brutally murdered their families. Who practically bathed in the blood of every human he ever encountered. "You are a worthless coward. A monster. A murderer, a torturer, a cruel and merciless king who—"

He cuts me off with an elegantly raised hand, rings glittering on half his fingers. "Yes, yes. I've been called many colorful names over the millennia, most of them unkind, however true they may be. But I've another name, as well. A name not a single soul has *ever* uttered aloud." His smile turns icy. He lifts a lock of my hair, pressing it to his mouth and inhaling deeply. "It's an honor reserved solely for you."

The chill in his voice sinks deep into my bones. My heart. My very soul.

And I know. Before he even speaks the words, I know.

"You, my moon," he continues, "may call me Father."

Thank you so much for reading Wicked Devouring!

After Westlyn's devastating capture—not to mention the ticking clock on the gargoyle curse and the terrifying implications of the Moon Blessed prophecy—everything is on the line for our dark fae witch and her fiercely possessive mates!

Find out what happens next in **Wicked Ascending, the fourth and final book of the Claimed by Gargoyles series.**

But first... have you grabbed your free bonus book, A Gargoyle Obsessed, featuring that hot, devoted psycho Jude Hendrix?

Sign up for my newsletter and you'll receive your copy. This story takes place the night Jude first meets his sweet little scarecrow in the park, and it can't be found anywhere else—it's an exclusive gift just for my subscribers. And it's available in ebook AND audio narrated by Shane East!

Can't see the link? Visit SarahPiperBooks.com/jude to claim your copy.

~

Are you a member of our private Facebook group, Sarah Piper's Sassy Witches? Pop in for sneak peeks, cover reveals, exclusive giveaways, book chats, group therapy to deal with these killer cliffhangers, and plenty of complete randomness from your fellow fans! We'd love to see you there.

LOOKING FOR AUDIOBOOKS?

A New Way to Get Your Audio Fix...

Audiobook lovers, you can now buy audiobooks directly from my author store at **SarahPiperBooks.com/shop** for early access and huge savings!

The books will still be available on other retailers like Audible and Apple, but buying direct means you can:

• **Save big.** Author store prices are 30-60% off retail prices.

• **Be the first to listen.** New releases will typically be available for direct buy for advanced release 1-2 weeks before they hit other retailers.

• **Directly support your favorite authors and narrators.** Your support means the world to me, and helps ensure I can continue to partner with the best narrators in the industry to bring these stories to life!

Visit SarahPiperBooks.com/shop to get started!

MORE BOOKS FROM SARAH PIPER!

Looking for more Reverse Harem romance?

THE WITCH'S REBELS is a reverse harem series featuring five smoldering-hot guys and the kickass witch they'd kill to protect (yes, you may be sensing a theme here)! If you like dark magic, sexy, forbidden romance, and heart-pounding supernatural thrills, this witchy adventure will leave you spellbound!

TAROT ACADEMY is a university-aged reverse harem paranormal academy romance starring four seriously hot mages and one badass witch. Dark prophecies, unique Tarot mythology, steamy romance (of course!), and plenty of supernatural suspense make this series a must-read!

In the mood for some naughty vampires instead?

Get bitten by the
VAMPIRE ROYALS OF NEW YORK!

DARK DECEPTION kicks off Dorian and Charlotte's story, a scorching vampire romance trilogy featuring a dirty-talking vampire king reluctant to take the throne after his father's demise and the seductive thief who might just bring him to ruin... or become his eternal salvation.

HEART OF THORNS is the first in Gabriel and Jacinda's series, a trilogy starring an ice-cold vampire prince and the witch he's captured from his enemy—the only person who can break his family's blood curse. Gabriel is Dorian's youngest brother, and his story picks up right where Dorian's ends.

ABOUT SARAH PIPER

Sarah Piper is a witchy, Tarot-card-slinging paranormal romance and urban fantasy author. Through her signature brew of dark magic, heart-pounding suspense, and steamy romance, Sarah promises a sexy, supernatural escape into a world where the magic is real, the monsters are sinfully hot, and the witches always get their magically-ever-afters.

Readers have dubbed her work "super sexy," "imaginative and original," "off-the-walls good," and "delightfully wicked in the best ways," a quote Sarah hopes will appear on her tombstone.

Originally from New York, Sarah now makes her home in northern Colorado with her husband (though that changes frequently) (the location, not the husband), where she spends her days sleeping like a vampire and her nights writing books, casting spells, gazing at the moon, playing with her ever-expanding collection of Tarot cards, binge-watching Supernatural (Team Dean!), and obsessing over the best way to brew a cup of tea.

You can find her online at SarahPiperBooks.com, on TikTok at @sarahpiperbooks, and in her Facebook readers group at Sarah Piper's Sassy Witches! If you're sassy, or if you need a little *more* sass in your life, or if you need more Dean Winchester gifs in your life (who doesn't?), come hang out!

Made in the USA
Monee, IL
25 June 2024

60460223R00173